## Acknowledgments

I would like to thank the following for their contributions in bringing this book to life. I am deeply indebted to them all.

Agent/Alchemist: Rob McQuilkin

Editor/Essentialist: Tina Pohlman

Heir Apparent: Nate Knaebel

Legal Tenders: Jonathan Reiss, David Stephens

Visual Aids: David Armstrong, Julie Lee, Ed Parrinello

Hearth & Home: Jack and Laurie Heflin

Steering Committee: Arthur Nersesian, Nicholas Shrady, Liam Burke, Jack Walworth, Sue Anthony, Sigrid Estrada, Peter Kloehn, Clemens Frischenschlager, Andrew Littell

Tea & Sympathy: Rachel and Ben Elwes, Emily Thing, Consuelo and Paolo (RIP) Mariniello, Adelina Bissolo, Floriana Campanozzi, Laurence Ceuzin, Piera Grandesso

For my parents,
Robert and Nancy Johnston

The past is never dead, it's not even the past.

—William Faulkner

'80

# '80

Whit Johnston

CARROLL & GRAF PUBLISHERS
NEW YORK

*'80*

Carroll & Graf Publishers
An Imprint of Avalon Publishing Group Inc.
245 West 17th Street
New York, NY 10011

AVALON
publishing group incorporated

First Carroll & Graf edition 2004

Library of Congress Cataloging-in-Publication Data is available.

ISBN: 0-7867-1398-4

Printed in the United States of America
Interior design by Paul Paddock
Distributed by Publishers Group West

'80

# Introduction

Chances are you've never heard of Mary Louise Weeks. You are not alone. If Mary Louise, or M. L. as she preferred to be called, was an important though unrecognized photographer, she was also the original postmodern diarist. What I have chosen to call, simply, *'80* is not only a deliciously bent first-person account of a young Manhattan artist trying her best to be "on the make," but also a vital rendering of a zeitgeist with everyone from John Lennon to street pornographer Ugly George along for the ride.

For a city that no longer prides itself on its hard-won perversity, 1980 New York can seem an Ice Age away. Weeks's power to evoke this colorful lost sliver of time— one not yet perhaps given its proper historical due—stands alone as a singular achievement in the diarist tradition, pomo or otherwise.

By way of introduction, the period covered here was marked by profound cultural and political shifts coupled with a preponderance of ends: the end of the permanence of Art, the end of the Underground, and perhaps most profoundly, the end of the authentic. (President-elect Ronald Reagan would not, after all, become our president but rather an actor elected to *play* our president.) In short, Modernism as we knew it was over, and with it, one could argue, the twentieth century.

By 1980, time and space were becoming increasingly

irrelevant. If satellites were shrinking our world (and our attention span) then the Betamax and its videotape were rendering it non-linear and fragmented. The more choices we were given, the more restless we became—McLuhan's Global Village was gradually transmogrifying into a cantankerous simulacra of the Tower of Babel.

It was in this void then, that The United States of Entertainment, the place we now call home, would first be given form. Strange new mutations like music videos, twenty-four-hour news cycles (CNN's "nuzak") and an ever-rising obsession with celebrity culture began to surface, ensuring that our senses would never again need be dulled by the white noise of dead air. With the double yoke of an increase in both leisure time and disposable income placed firmly around our necks, we were destined to become little more than what we indeed *have* become: a Prozac/TV/Jackass Nation steeped in easy irony and world-weary sighs. Captive audience no more, we now live with more choices than we can process, at a pace we can't possibly maintain—a country of impatient children. It's difficult sometimes to remember that life wasn't always as such.

While Weeks came of age in the embers of post-literate sixties anger ("The Peace and Pollution Revolution" as she refers to it here), by the time of these entries she was clearly rediscovering the power of the written word, something she had first latched onto as an English Lit major at Barnard. A quiet, recoiling type in her private life, she was a woman transformed when she picked up a camera. At haunts of the flesh like the Canal Street Piers, Plato's Retreat, and The Saint, Weeks was there, front and center for the closing hours of The Last Great Party, where the private was made public with Dionysian abandon and the edges of human sexuality and drug use were explored as a matter of course. ("Gay Cancer"—as the dreaded HIV virus was dubbed early on— would not surface for another year.)

Those of us who were familiar with the extremes of Weeks's methods alternately marveled and worried about her public brazenness, given the unpredictable, hair-trigger tempera-ment of most New Yorkers. Her explanation of her own safety was, as always, perverse. In her mind, New Yorkers were the only people in the world who *would* allow her to come so close. In a city where simply riding the subway can be a test of one's personal space, tolerance is not so much a quality as a necessary survival tool. Nothing surprises them for, as she liked to claim, if you stand on a Manhattan corner long enough, one of everything can and probably *will* walk by.

Undaunted when working in her beloved Manhattan, she was also obsessed by it, in much the same way Joyce was with Dublin, though, unlike the great Irish writer, exile was not a viable option for her. "When you leave New York, I don't care where you're headed, you're on your way to nowhere," was her patented response when asked why she never took a vacation.

If one had to place her historically in the pantheon of influential photographers, she was the redheaded stepchild of Diane Arbus and Robert Frank, the incestuous daughter of William Klein, the salacious sister of Robert Mapplethorpe. Had M. L. been a war photog—and she would have made a great one—she'd no doubt be as famous as Robert Capa, and probably just as dead.

Dismissive of those she saw as sheep-like "all-swallowers," she was not so much a cultural pessimist as a hard-edged, urban dweller long on opinions and not afraid to share them. The writing contained herein wends its way from the intensely personal to the rigidly sacrosanct, from the joyfully irreverent to the downright accusatory, all of it infused with a wide-eyed earnestness that somehow does not preclude a world-weary skepticism far beyond her twenty-eight years. Weeks answers in these pages, it seems, James's call for an aesthetic of "felt life," firm in the belief that she could feel more deeply than anyone who ever lived, as only a twenty-something *can* believe.

Biting social criticism and a photographer's eye for detail make this an indispensable reading of a pivotal transitional moment in New York history and the culture at large. For those of you who were of age in 1980, this will hopefully reengage you with that seminal moment in American history. For those too young to remember (or not yet born!) may you take inspiration in these pages written just before the onset of creeping commercialism, and indeed our collective national Alzheimer's.

If a psychiatrist is someone who knows nothing and does nothing, and a surgeon is someone who knows nothing and does everything, then a pathologist is the person who knows everything but is always a day or two late. With the publication of these journals, M. L. Weeks takes her place as one of the preeminent social pathologists of her time, a time before we knew we wanted our MTV, before Absolut *Any*thing. Drink up!

Marvin Schagrin
President and CEO, State of the Fine Art Gallery
Executor, The Estate of M. L. Weeks
www.mlweeks.net

**N.B.:** The diary of M. L. Weeks was found by her estranged husband in a mattress some twenty years after it was written. I have chosen to present the pages here unexpurgated. The entry headings are my own addition, poetic license which I am certain M. L. not only would have granted but warmly embraced.

SUMMER '80

### Rising to the Bait
August 22, 1980

It's one in the morning and I've just returned from my last Attica run. Feeling like the waitress who's finally home and idle after a double shift but the tyranny of routine keeps her scanning the apartment for empty water glasses and dirty ashtrays. Totally wired.

Haven't had the compulsion to keep a diary, journal, *cahier*, whatever they are calling them these days since just after college, before it became clear the last thing the world needed was another self-important, fresh-faced English major convinced of her own opinions. But with B's departure, this loft, much like this life, feels unspeakably barren. And so I write.

But whom do I tell when I tell a blank page, Virginia? Those Barnard journals still irk, how I held them up like a talisman to guard against all the collegial good-fellowship, all that "sisterhood" bearing down. The unexamined life may not be worth living, but that essentially "unlived" university life surely wasn't deserving of the audit given to it in those endless pages.

Would like to think I could put *these* pages to better use, to perhaps free myself of even the most entrenched self-deceptions I've been clinging to for the better part of my post-adolescent life. Truth be told, reliable narration of my own life's line has never been a personal strength—why should this little exercise be any less disingenuous?

Writing is supposed to help you find out how you feel, no? Well I know how I feel—I feel like shit. We lived together, B and I, in an undivided, self-perpetuating vacuum. It certainly wasn't ideal, but it was good enough to want to make it better, to stick around. I really didn't need anyone else. Were I to cop to the sheer helplessness I'm feeling at the moment, staring down the prospect of being alone long term, I'd feel a little too much like Didi and Gogo at the hanging tree to even *begin* to argue the possibility of going on.

Bleaker than Beckett, now there's something to crow about. Reminds me of those earnest, endless Sartre vs. Camus debates we used to try and impress each other with at Spence. No collection of "alienated little me" diatribes this, no romancing the misery, I promise. What's that Basic Training cant . . . ? Pain is a sensation and all sensations are to be enjoyed. Every masochist needs a sadist and I obviously found mine, tra-la, tra-la!

Lest we forget, there is nothing even remotely romantic about a blank piece of paper, particularly when yellow and lined. These legal pads, the ones I intend to fill, have been mocking me from the nightstand, daring me to remove their shrink-wrap and hold forth since the day B left them (and me) behind. But that was three months ago, why rise to the bait tonight?

Maybe this fucking heat has had me stewing in my own juices so long I've become delusional about my powers of observation. Or maybe it's that surge of energy (if not necessarily inspiration) that follows a serious breakup once the crying jags have ebbed. Maybe. More to the point is my dire need for distraction, some semblance of R-E-L-I-E-F from this *crie de coeur* tape loop running around my squirreled brain, ad nauseam.

No doubt, I should be throwing myself into one social swirl or another, washing the proverbial man right out of the proverbial hair. Unfortunately, I seem to have neither the inclination nor patience for the company of others. It all reads as so much quick-fix folly. The very thought of having to recultivate old friendships and/or form new ones just makes me tired. With the possible exception of Mary, there isn't a single person out there I could countenance right now, not one.

So I continue to surround myself with myself, keeping my own best company, trying to revel in the sleep of the just, knowing everyone else is either wrong or irrelevant. I sound like one of Fyodor's "insulted and injured" for Christ's sake, but it's true. I have, to put it bluntly, painted myself into a very empty shell of a corner. If we are indeed forever stuck trying to recreate that first place we felt comfortable enough to call "home," then it's back to square one for this wayfaring stranger. How's that for brutal self-evaluation?

Sooner or later we all need to know we've been absolved. Catholics have their confessional, communists their circles of self-criticism, and the rest of us are left to sweat our personal poisons out on the couches of headshrinkers . . . or simply swallow. Which brings us back to these foolish yellow pads.

Always believed words and images created irreconcilable versions of the same world. Gave up my writerly ambitions because I preferred the illusion of the image to the reality of sentences and exclamation points. Now I'm not sure what to believe. What I *do* know is that taking pictures and composing paragraphs are both acts of *faith*, something I don't have a whole lot of at the moment. Maybe tomorrow.

### Stewed
August 26, 1980
12:20 P.M.

This bloody heat wave has made itself a little too comfortable. ("Bloody," is it? I resent these fucking Briticisms that have seeped into my vocab, yet one more spectre of B The Not-So-Friendly Ghost.)

The city is stewing under a vermilion haze, one of those thermal inversions no one likes to talk about. While the hardier souls press on with the day's routine, the more delicate flowers among us hunker down with our air conditioners and iced coffees, waiting for nightfall to cool off all this brick and cement.

(Note: Have decided to include the time of day of each entry—more accurate, no?)

Only the cook from the Chinese beneath me seems happy in this soup, probably because he knows the G-12's down at Immigration won't be planning any raids in humidity this evil. I hear him in the back alley now, hacking his way through another cigarette while the moo shu simmers. At least I *think* that's what I smell coming through the floorboards. Reminiscent of the curried mornings I used to wake up to living above the Bengalis back on 6th Street, albeit not quite as pungent. Wise old Marvin once tried to tell me that none of the seven Chinese dialects have a word for "solitude." If I didn't believe him then, I certainly take his point now.

I suppose I could still escape to Woodstock with Mary this weekend but the prospect of enduring more sordid details of her d-i-v-o-r-c-e will probably keep me off that train. Last week she let one out of the bag I still can't quite believe. Apparently, when Leon told her it was over—that he was leaving her for another woman—Mary's reaction was to pull him into bed for one last go.

"I wanted to make sure he'd never forget what he was giving up—we had a very strong sexual connection, you know."

Know? It would be hard *not* to know, given all the talk of penis dimensions and multiple orgasms I've had to endure from her over the years. Relishing more than your share of little deaths is one thing, gloating about them to your friends quite another.

One can usually size up a potential lover from the way they eat. That Leon attacked his food like the unblinking snake he was, leads me to doubt mutually-satisfying sex was ever at the fulcrum of whatever it was that kept those two together so long.

As loathsome as it may sound, I hung up the phone after this last Mary disclosure, strangely elated by her need to rationalize it to me, as if it had somehow attenuated my own romantic bunglings. Taking solace in another's pain—a terrible thing to do to someone who calls you a friend but then it wouldn't be the first time, would it?

Note yet another annoying idiomatic Briticism: that compulsion to turn every thought into a question as if voicing a simple declarative sentence would be considered what . . . too presumptuous? It's that false modesty/stiff upper lip syndrome I loved so to mock in B and his Oxbridge ilk.

B once told me a story from his tour-guide days in which he was taking a group of "adventurers" from dear ole Blighty to the Valley of the Kings, the final leg of which was done on donkey. Just before reaching their destination, he noticed one of the wives was so terrified of her animal that she'd been crapping herself to the point where the stuff was now slithering down her legs. Rather than draw attention to herself, however, the poor thing chose to suffer in stoic silence, rubbing it into her skin, hoping no one would notice. Everyone did, of course, yet no mention of it was ever made, not even behind her back.

Even if her fear of the donkey was perfectly well-founded, I can't imagine taking one's inner fortitude to such an extreme. Perhaps that's what B expects of me, to just keep absorbing (if not in fact, *eating*) his shit in stoic silence. Not I, the grin-and-bear-it kind, mister, no matter how low my self-esteem.

### Dismantled/Dissembling

August 27, 1980

11:15 A.M.

After refusing to sleep in our bed since the departure of the dear departed one, I've finally taken the thing apart piece by four-poster piece, banishing it to the darkroom. I was tired of looking at it, tired of the failure and deceit it represented, tired of being reminded how foolish yet helpless one feels when emotions begin to cathect onto objects. Anyway, the less furniture, the cleaner the lines of the loft, and, theoretically at least, the less cluttered my pretty little head. Am I turning Japanese or is this hankering for simplicity just some perverse, faux nostalgia for a fab '60s experience I never had?

B knows I want the bed out of here, but he also knows I won't put it on the street, just like he knows I'm not going to divorce him, turn him over to the INS, stick him for his half of the rent, etc., etc. Meanwhile, he and his cupcake continue to hide behind his new answering machine (quite the invention, that!), neatly keeping at bay the guilt the very sound of my voice must evoke.

So here I lie, wrenching my already wrenched back on the pullout couch out of some misguided sense of principle. (Whoever had the design innovation to place a bar across the center of these things obviously never had to sleep on one.) It's a little late to be invoking principle, I realize, but when the beloved has now bought the very machine he forbade me to buy so that he can now screen *my* calls, any victory is welcomed, however Pyrrhic.

Now would be a good time to start printing from the stack of negs accumulating across the room, but no can do, Kemo Sabe . . . the bed is in the darkroom. Another act of self-sabotage? Perhaps. But who of consequence does their own printing anymore, anyway? And if you subscribe to the conceit that we create to attract the opposite sex, then printing is definitely the last thing I want to do right now. Besides, the smell of fixer would only make me more nauseated than I already am.

The sadness *is* beginning to dissipate, it's mostly longing now. Not desirous, not for sex necessarily, but for some sort of intimate connection, some kind of communion. And confusion, above all else there is confusion. When what begins as a friendship alchemizes into something deeper, then ends abruptly, I guess it's to be expected.

Maybe it was the proximity—you spend enough time together and the companionship, the familiarity, is too easily mistaken for something else, something more magnificent. B was a warm bath, clean comfort. I fell into the swirl of him without even knowing it, yet also never completely gave myself over, half-expecting him to do at any moment the very thing he eventually did. So I knew. I knew. Like most love this one, too, went unrequited. But how many relationships are about love anyway? Love, real love, seems an elusive creature all its own, and one I'm not sure I've even known.

With B, it all begins and ends with the money. There are times when I feel like turning him in for overstating the obvious, for making a mockery of our travesty. Perhaps if I hadn't let him pay me, if it was merely a favor from one *friend* to another, things would have been more balanced, if somewhat less spectacular, without that wonderfully inappropriate sex-for-hire undercurrent that informed our lovemaking or fucking or whatever the hell it was we thought we were doing.

Either way, marriage is *always* an exchange, some kind of quid pro quo in one form or another, be it monetary, emotional, intellectual, whatever. Two people wanting, or at least *thinking*, they need what the other one has in order to complete themselves. B's "needs," if that's what we're to call them, were just a bit more *immediate* than mine, i.e., he *need*ed to be able to stay in the country.

Perhaps if I had been more candid about my own emotions he wouldn't have "proposed." No surprise then that he was so insistent about paying me—it's what gave him the clean out, the guilt-free right to beat the retreat, wily Englishman that he is. "Wily Englishman," if that isn't a tautology. In the grander scheme, what really disturbs is how men and women seem to be able to miss each other so entirely. To wit: a man and a woman kiss. He thinks she's ready for sex, she thinks he's ready for marriage. A pox on the medieval House of France for ever coming up with such a ludicrous concept as romantic love in the first place—it's so . . . impractical . . . I haven't the time and I certainly don't have the constitution. I'd rather be treated as chattel, or better yet, simply left alone. Now there's an idea.

**Haiku**
August 28, 1980
2:55 P.M.
Ran into an old beau outside Murray's this morning. The entire exchange was so brief I'm still not sure it happened— just as well if I looked anything like I felt.

I'm waiting in line with my cheese and through the window out on the street is a guy doing a balancing act with a stack of books so high they obscure his face. He keeps rapping at the window, motioning for me to come out. Only when I finally make it outside do I recognize him; Oliver Cushing from Collegiate, the first boy I ever spent the entire night with.

No time for pleasantries apparently, as he launches right into it. Mindlessly working his way up some white-shoe law firm (Sullivan & Cromwell?), he's leaving the Columbus Circle station one rush-hour night and feels something sharp in his back. Looking down, he sees his blue pinstripe saturating to red.

Next thing he remembers is waking up in the hospital where his mother hands him a copy of himself on the cover of the *Post*, splayed on the ground, unconscious. Says he made up his mind right then and there when he saw that picture that he was not "going out an effin lawyer," quits his job and has spent the last six months reading the Great American Novels. Next week it's off to Paris to write one of his own.

And that was it. He was gone, back to the library, turning in his read stack for a new one. No time even for the awkward

"Do we exchange phones numbers or not?" interlude. The whole encounter was like living inside a perfect haiku.

## Don't Feed Me
August 29, 1980
4:25 P.M.

Trying to come up with some new portrait/essay ideas, work I can submit for the next round of NEAs. Was thinking about doing something on cocaine—decadence as socially tolerated recreation—but finally thought it too ironic, like cultivating a cynical appreciation of disco to use as cocktail chatter at insufferable parties.

Very debilitating, all this internal backing-and-forthing. The indecision can be endless, the curse of a rational mind. Some say objectivity is artistic arsenic masquerading as open-mindedness, but there is always going to be this problem of ultimately having to make a choice, Kierkegaard's eternal *Either/Or*: "If I don't marry this woman I will regret it and if I do marry this woman I will regret it." That poor bastard died bent over and alone, which should tell me *something*, exactly what, I know not.

Self-doubt has its role in the creative equation to be sure, but it can bring on involuntary indolence. If an idea doesn't smack of possibility I want to try and let go of it as quickly as I possibly can. The less time wasted debating amongst one's various selves, the sooner one gets to the crux. What you want is something that jumps down your throat and makes you feel the fool not to swallow. Like the women and children that night huddled at Columbus Circle, waiting for the bus to take them to see their husbands/fathers in Attica. When they told me what they were waiting for, I knew instinctively I had to go with them. Only later did I consider the implications of my imposition.

Or when the pathologist friend of B's dad first floated the possibility of shooting in a morgue, intuition alone set me in motion. Not once did I stop to consider what shooting the dead might actually *entail*, the physical/psychological toll, people's response to the transgression, etc. Had I weighed those factors, I probably never would have done it, and spared myself the vitriol; but if you always know where it is you're going, why ever would you want to go there? It's clear now the negative reaction invoked by that series was more about the viewer's attitude toward death than the work itself. If anything, it was a Rorschach for gauging one's comfort level with what awaits.

Something did actually catch my eye yesterday as I was absently thumbing through the *Sunday Times Magazine*. In the back, beneath a preposterously priced Fairfield County Colonial, was a small ad featuring a disgruntled, chubby preteen girl and the exhortation: "Girls! Add it Up: Weight Loss + New Friends = Fun, Fun, Fun." No testimonials, no faked before-and-afters, just a slippery promise and an upstate phone number.

A fat camp for twelve-year-olds—is this something new? Guess it's never too early to start a girl obsessing over her weight. Remake/remodel, the culture of perfectibility. Tell me more, tell me more! More to the point, let me shoot you. Have a call in to the Diet Mistress and fingers crossed.

## 11:55 P.M. . . . Can't Sleep

Fantastically horny, have been all day. Having anything even *resembling* a sexual impulse feels like no small feat since hitting the wall with B. Letting my fingers do the walking is falling short—it only gets me more het up, which requires more friction, which . . . and 'round and 'round we go. I'm stranded in the Land of the Frustrates, that fetid glen between heightened arousal and insatiate desire. Help!

## Will Work for Food

August 30, 1980

11:33 P.M.

Labor Day already this weekend—the summer will soon be gone and with it my excuses for not chasing down more work. Nothing irks like having to suck up to self-absorbed art directors, particularly those of the anarchist black and severely angled hair, the uniform of choice these days among the Condé Nasties et al. All that dickering and for what—$250 a page? I'm better off going back to waiting tables.

It's their meekness, the utter spinelessness that grates—cannibalizing each other's ideas until fresh blood finally breaks through the stranglehold and the (auto)phaging process can begin anew. Like the swirl surrounding D. Turbeville. She turns out an interesting spread or two, something we haven't exactly seen before, and suddenly everything has to be awash in sepia-toned, faux urban decadence. Fashion as nostalgia. Nostalgia for what . . . the Victorians? That first orgasm?

The whole (mis)representation of "models" as iconographic begs credulity if you've seen enough of them in person. Magazines use models not because they're more beautiful than the average bear—they're not—but because everything about a successful model, feature-wise at least, is exaggerated. From her height, to the angles of her face, she is, in fact, a human caricature who on the printed page appears not only normal but actually *desirable*. Why? Because the camera lies, exquisitely. If the women who buy these slicks could actually see these girls in the flesh they'd probably feel much less inadequate about themselves and much less inclined to buy into whatever product/lifestyle was being pushed on the page.

As the photographer, manipulating self-esteem is, in essence, the tacit assignment you're given when hired. But if I'm going to shoot a model it's not going to be about impossible desirability, but about intimacy. I'm not projecting *onto* them, I'm identifying *with* them, trying to tap into some quality I see in them which I recognize in myself, and expanding on it. That is exactly what you will get if you hire me, so there's no point in giving these editors what they think they want, if what they think they want isn't what I do, if that makes any sense. I'll just lose interest and the work will suffer accordingly.

But really—why should these editors hire me? They're better off giving the assignment to some young buck who is not only easy to direct (read: manipulate) but may even, if only as a professional courtesy, respond to their craven attempts at seduction.

Editorial doesn't pay and commercial work's a bore. It's times like these when I think the Depression-era photogs—the Evans and Langes of the world—really had the life. With little if any commercial work available, the temptation for a money grab was eliminated, your path was effectively chosen for you. Couldn't very well "sellout" if there was no one there to sellout to, now could you? And while nobody was getting rich, they all seemed to be able to get by (FSA and otherwise), *and* keep doing work that mattered to them. Who amongst us dare ask for more?

Not I. Gets very tedious, this incessant fret over where the next paycheck may or may not be coming from. The limit is having to explain myself and my choices to those for whom work is little more than a means to an end, i.e., making money for the sake of making money. Little wonder everyone you see shuffling around Midtown looks so miserable half the time. Why do you think they call it a job?

Wonder how much more parental shit I'll have to eat for taking the freelancer route? Hell, until the Industrial Revolution *everyone* was a freelancer. Thought that was the *raison d'être* of a good liberal arts education, to allow the individual to make free choices in a free society. If the 'rents were so intent on my being a wage slave they should have sent me to vocational school.

A holiday like tomorrow's only serves to agitate and remind how twisted our whole concept of "labor" has become. We've made work the centerpiece of our lives to the point where we have a hard time even introducing ourselves to others without asking them what they do. We need those education and income cues to know how to make sense of someone.

Everywhere else it's considered rude to ask someone you've just met such a question, but here it's usually the first thing that pops out, the proverbial icebreaker that immediately determines if the conversation will go anywhere or if it's time to freshen up your drink.

So what exactly *is* it I do when not busy thinking about the pictures I'm not taking and the money I'm not making? Nothing, how about nothing? I do *nothing*! Wonder how that would go down at the next soirée?

Personally, I blame Martin Luther for taking it upon himself to convince the world that not working should be considered morally corrupt, that the unemployed and/or unemployable are good-for-nothings. Before he arrived on the scene, beggars and the poor were given first dibs in line at the pearly gates. Remember? What, pray tell, Mister Luther, became of the meek inheriting the earth? Not that I'm planning *quite* that far ahead, mind you, but is that still on, or what?

Lest the day be *completely* given over to idle rant and rumination, I actually set out this morning on my bike for the upper reaches of Central Park. Exercise was the excuse but I was also determined to find some young Latino toughs beating the heat in their tube shirts and cutoffs, maybe get them to pose for me. Those sculpted bodies adorned with ornate tattoos and gold chains . . . a highlight of any New York summer.

My trip is diverted somewhere around 14th Street, however, when I cross paths with some joker wearing one those new "personal" mini-stereos. Lost in his own private globule of song, he crosses into me and I swerve into a sinkhole to avoid him and over the handlebars me goes, Nikons and all. Bleeding from the knees, I scramble to my feet and head for home but not before coming across a police horse passed out on the sidewalk by Sheridan Square, a "wictim" (as Dagmar used to say) of heat prostration.

Am busy soaking my wounds in a cold bath, thoroughly defeated and obsessing over the poor horse, when Kertesz starts giving my cuts palliative licks, although he may just have been playing up to me in hopes of scarfing a bite or two of my sandwich. God knows I love this dog, I just wish sometimes he would go off on his own and do whatever it is a dog is supposed to do instead of always staring at me for his next cue. And it's only gotten worse since B's departure.

Kertesz is attached to me, I'm still attached to B, and the roundelay continues. Wish I had more the personality of a cat, that I became attached to places rather than people.

Far easier to get along I should think, if not necessarily as satisfying.

## State of Our Union

Labor Day, 1980
7:05 P.M.

In a country where beating the USSR in hockey has supposedly revived the collective national self-image ("Do you believe in miracles?"), I know I'm living in Manhattan for a reason, namely that it's an island *off the coast* of America.

Not poor Jimmy Carter, alas. He's thoroughly mired in the belly of the beast, and it's all turning rather ghastly for him, I'm afraid. Hostages still in Tehran, Soviets still in Afghanistan, and now Peter Jennings says the Ku Klux Klan has put a price on Carter's presidential head for "selling out the white man." If that's not enough, the guy now has to hit the campaign trail and try to appear as if he really wants another four years of all this.

On the subway today, kids with a boom box were blasting that song "Bomb Iran, Bomb Iran" (done to the tune of the Beach Boy's "Barbara Ann") until our very own band of homegrown vigilantes, a.k.a. the Guardian Angels, made them turn it off. A few stops later, a Bowery flophouser stumbles into the car and starts in on how hard it is to find good Russian vodka these days what with the boycott and I'm thinking: if I were Carter I'd be thinking about pulling an LBJ ("I shall not seek, nor will I accept the nomination of my party for a second term as your President . . .") right about now. Life back there in Plains with Ma Kettle and Billy Beer never looked so good, I should think.

But, tonight, there was Jiminy on Jennings, sweating through his shirtsleeves, pressing the flesh in some godforsaken

Alabama swampland with former Gov. George "I'm-Still-Here" Wallace, who, from a wheelchair no less, managed to smother the standing president in an unctuous bear hug. Carter froze before falling onto Wallace's lap, knowing it was what the locals of Cabbageville had been waiting for but also well aware it was one photo-op that would play as political poison everywhere else in the country.

The grimace on Mister President's face was palpable, as if he were a ten-year-old about to go under the rubella umbrella for the first time. When Wallace finally released him, the poor man's eyes were stinging with sweat, his flimsy façade of confidence all but melted. George Wallace as the new Killer Rabbit. *That's* entertainment.

Reagan's handlers, meanwhile, concocted the picture-perfect Labor Day scenario for their boy over in Jersey, in some place called, fittingly enough, "Liberty Park." Framed on one side by the Manhattan skyline and Lady Liberty on the other, "The Man Who Time Forgot" spoke in lofty, meaningless aphorisms about freedom and prosperity using the backdrop as not-too-terribly-subliminal reinforcement for his "message," such as it was. Without breaking a sweat the guy managed to look, well, "presidential," or at least more so than the president.

Carter must be doing *something* right to get the GOP so firmly planted behind so far-right a relic as Reagan, but, perish the thought, what if the wizened old huckster should actually *win*? May very well be time to dig out my old high school French books from the maid's room uptown. I, for one, haven't the social skills (much less the wardrobe) for a country turned Republican.

## A Day in the Country
September 3, 1980
9:52 A.M.

Too much has happened since last entry but will try and lay it out as best I can.

It took a certain untruth but was finally able to set up a shoot at the fat camp. (Told them I was doing a spread on today's youth for *Life*, which I later learned is about to fold, if it hasn't already.) After a wrong turn off the NY State Thruway, I manage to improvise my way there by the appointed hour. Following a quick tour of the grounds—wonderfully rambling but in need of some serious TLC—I start shooting the fifty or so campers lunching on some kind of low-fat, cottage-cheesy concoction they're washing down with a syrupy-red bug juice. Apparently fat is out, pure sugar is OK. My kind of diet.

In a gesture borne more of self-interest than gratitude, I offer to take three of the more ungainly misses to a nearby lake I passed on the way out. Diet Mistress agrees only after I promise no side trips to ice cream shacks or any other such roadside confectioneries that fleck the landscape up there this time of year. A mile in, it's a broken promise, and the girls are all mine.

Our afternoon's going well enough: I have them swim out to a raft, put them up in a rotting lifeguard's chair, there is some horseplay, etc., nothing unusual until on the way out we see a sign we managed to miss on the way in: "Swimming Area Closed"—High E. coli Count." I assure them they won't die until *after* the big good-bye dance with the boys' fat camp across the lake, which seems to quell their fears right up until we hit the deer.

Someone (Stravinsky?) once claimed we experience time in one of three modes: ontologically, psychologically, and the same way in which we encounter art. Hitting that poor deer seemed to encompass all three.

As I play it back, I recall something resembling an appeal for reassurance settling across the stricken animal's visage moments after appearing on the hood. Our eyes lock and we study each other through the cracked windshield for what seems a short eternity before I eventually find the presence of mind to pull over.

My first reaction (surprise!) is to grab a camera, the one with the Tri-X. The girls cowering in the backseat, their milkshakes strewn across the floorboards, the injured animal splayed across the front of the car—everything, I shoot everything.

"You killed it!" snipes one.

The beached deer kicks a hind leg out every so often, making sure I haven't forgotten her.

"Oeuwwwww—it's not even dead . . ." cries another.

Clearly, this was the deep end of the pool—blood, trauma, screaming girls—it was enough to turn one primal; fight or flight time. Part of me, a very *large* part in fact, wants to do just that, wants to grab my things and run, far, far away down that cursed, Frostian country road. My little horse must think it queer, indeed.

The voyeur in me proves more rooted than the coward, and I keep shooting, but my fixation with the camera only serves to distress the girls more. How could I continue to snap away when there is a very large, very bloodied animal in the throes of death thrashing around on our hood?

To them, I've hit Bambi and now I have to put her back the way she was, make her right, as if that's part of the social contract between child and adult, making sure all in the world is right. And yes, as the lone adult, I *should* be offering some kind of reassurance, something along the lines of, "It's OK girls, the poor deer may well be bleeding within inches of her life *now* but not to worry, she'll soon rise up from this sorry state and bound her way back into the woods where family and other concerned animal kingdom friends are preparing a 'Welcome Home' filled with dancing and singing and carrying on."

But everything is *not* going to be all right and they know it. We are decidedly fucked and my silence, my abdication of responsibility as the lone authority figure, is leaving the girls confused and vulnerable. They begin to act out, loudly demanding I fix it, put it back the way it was, that I do *some*thing . . . ! (Could *this* be why I don't see myself having kids any time soon?)

"Kill it . . . you have to kill it . . ." bawls the largest girl, who by now looks ready to kill *me* if I don't do something.

And then, a small wonder, in the form of a Jeep arrives. A guy, probably my age, dressed in Army green with the physique of a convict is behind the wheel, surveying the situation, shaking his head. He's rather threatening looking, but then I think that of most of them upstate, the direct result of having been introduced to *Deliverance* at a far too impressionable age.

"How long ago this happen?"

He places himself between me and my catastrophe.

"Two, three minutes."

It was a guess, it could have been three hours, ask Stravinsky. He pulls the mother of all Bowie knives from somewhere and in one firm stroke bisects the deer's belly sending a steady wave of blood and entrails coursing down the hood and onto the road. Before it registers what has happened, the guy reaches into the breach and pulls out something not unlike the baby in *Eraserhead*, soaked in amniotic fluid and very much inanimate.

"Do me a favor and come over here."

Plainly, a man of few words—the strong-but-silent type. I put my camera around my neck and do as I'm told, only too happy to follow an order, any order. He hands me the newborn's hind legs and instructs I hold it upside down and shake, something about circulation and the blood-brain barrier. Fine by me, but soon the placenta is caught in the nostrils and it's starting to choke. Joe Buck wipes the viscous fluids from the newborn's face with his shirt, then jerks the faun a few times from its haunches, before gently setting it down on the grass apron.

Slowly the fawn comes to life, struggling to find its legs, trying to put itself upright, negotiating ever so tentatively this new world I have so violently forced upon it. By now traffic is backed up on both sides. No one is honking though, they are simply leaving their cars and silently marching toward us, *Dawn of the Dead*-like, inextricably drawn to the unfolding spectacle: the shell-shocked newborn straining for life in the grass, her gutted mother mercifully expired, body fluids pooled at her side. The cycle of life in one, bloody, god-awful eyeful.

Somehow calmed by the presence of other adults, I return to my camera and squeeze off a few more frames before the local dogcatcher arrives, carting off both newborn and carrion. I thank Scary Guy from the safety of the driver's seat, while the girls blithely wave their good-byes from the back. In the rearview I can make out his crooked, ambiguous smile, the one they flash just before they tell you to "Get them panties down!" I feel my foot press just a little bit harder on the gas.

The first thing to do after dropping the girls is replace the deer-damaged car. The nearest Avis is at the Watertown airport which means a rather dull hump, deeper into the soporific reaches of upstate. According to my map, the only hope for local diversion is a military school up near the Canadian border. With a little luck I can catch the new recruits and their parents streaming in for orientation. That was the idea at least.

The school, however, has apparently gone under with the election of Carter, this according to a local wag who, judging from his Reagan bumper sticker, isn't entirely impartial. I settle for lunch alfresco on the town's main thoroughfare and forget about it.

The waitress has just brought the check when I notice a camera crew at the opposite end of the street surrounded by a jostling crowd. Curious, I settle up and start toward them. It doesn't take long to see that at the center of the commotion is Barbara Walters, chit-chatting away with some guy I don't recognize. I start shooting the two of them in the eye of this human hurricane, trying to ignore the fact that Barbara's companion is doing his best to keep me from getting him, obscuring his face with his hands, turning his back, etc., until finally a producer-type approaches.

"Who's that with Barbara?" I ask, gently indulging my fondness for referring to celebrities by their first name.

"I can't tell you that, let's see some credentials."

"Don't have any."

"Who sent you?"

"No one . . ."

"You stringing . . ?"

"No . . ."

"Gimme it . . . gimme the film."

He lunges for the camera, I step back but right into the arms of another crew member who has slinked up behind me, copping a feel in the process. I call him a pig, slip his grip, and drift off toward the car. Satisfied I won't be back, the throng quickly regroups and carries on doing what they were doing before me and my camera intruded.

Fast-forward an hour or so to the mom-and-pop airport where I'm waiting in line for a new car when Baba appears again, this time trailed by a group of reporters who look on helplessly as her henchmen whisk her through the terminal, out onto the tarmac, and an awaiting charter. I learn from one of the hacks it's been leaked Baba has come to Tiny Town to interview '60s gadfly Abbie Hoffman, who has been AWOL (a.k.a. "underground") since trying to sell two pounds of cocaine to an FBI agent six years ago. No wonder my camera was so unwelcomed. I eighty-six the car and catch the next flight back to the city.

A phone call to a friend of Marvin's at ABC and the Abbie picture begins to resolve itself. Apparently, he really is ready to come in from the cold and is using Walters's show tomorrow night to announce it to the world. What better way to win public sympathy than a touchy-feely, tête-à-tête with America's favorite busybody. The guy always knew how to play the media but Baba Wawa?! Where's Gilda when you need her?!

Calls to the dailies start something of a bidding war—rumor of Abbie's imminent surfacing had already been circulating. I decide to go with the *Post* not because they offered the most (they didn't) but because they dangled the prospect of future assignments, if in fact I had what I said I had. I process the roll in question and run it down to South Street, so cranked I forget to do a contact.

According to one of the photo editors—Ben Jacobs, a massive man with a loaf of hair—I "nailed" it. Abbie looks agitated, like he clearly doesn't want his picture taken, which is exactly what the papers want and why whenever Madame Onassis tries to take a walk through Central Park under cover of Gucci scarf and dark glasses, we all know about it. Confronting the public beast and catching it off balance, out of character. The stolen shot. Pure gold.

So it's now off to the newsstand to feast over the fruit of accident. Perhaps I should use the $300 to buy a telephoto lens or maybe a motordrive, invest in my new "future." Shouldn't be so cynical—working for a tabloid just might save me from eating spoiled papaya on some godforsaken island listening to models debate the direction of next year's hemlines while we wait for the rain to stop. O, the paparazzi's life for me, tee-hee!

### Utopias Are for Losing

The Abbie floodgates have been flung open wide, the details and minutia of the missing years pouring in.

After going under the knife for a flattening of the nose and god knows what else, he eventually settles upstate near the St. Lawrence River as "Barry Freed, Clean-Water Activist Freelance Writer" (yet another hyphenated man), quickly winning over the neighbors, particularly the wives. With most husbands away at the office during the day, Barry is available to supervise play dates (his live-in has a young daughter), take UPS deliveries, and anything else that needs doing including whipping up a batch of his award-winning cranberry chutney. Who said life begins at forty . . . ?

What the housewives reported loving most about their neighbor was his "sunny disposition." He was always "up," "active," "full of energy," in sharp contrast, no doubt, to their own overworked husbands. Little wonder he was so sunny—probably had a stable of unhappily marrieds he was servicing on a regular basis. (Never trust anyone over thirty is right!) Cheating on your nine-to-five husband with a clean-water activist who turns out to be a famous sixties fugitive . . . there's one that's going to be hard to keep from the gals at the next bridge club.

Apparently, this has been timed to coincide with his putting out yet another autobiography which explains why he held a press conference at his publisher's office yesterday. A movie deal is also rumored, which must make him one of the select few wanted by both the FBI and Hollywood.

But perhaps there's something less obvious here than simple product pushing. Perhaps what drove him to turn himself in was a deep abiding need to put an end to the terrifically terrifyingly dull life he had managed to make for himself upstate: days besotted with Farmer Browns and church fairs, tractor pulls, and bake-offs. Perhaps laying low as a clean-water activist up there on that damn river was so interminably tedious that one day he just up and decided to see how blind justice really was in this country. To which I would defer to that old hate-monger Kipling: You're a better man than I am, Gunga Din.

If I sound cynical, it must be because I am. For starters, a captured fugitive does more time than one who turns himself in. More importantly though, for all their claims to the contrary, Abbie and his "New Left" friends represented little more than an extension of the *old* Left with one crucial difference: instead of coming of age in the Depression, they grew up in a country of unprecedented prosperity. Which is precisely why hippiedom always seemed such a crock to me; conspicuous consumption will always appear vulgar to those who want for nothing.

Even to my younger self, The Peace and Pollution Revolution appeared more petulant than revolutionary. What I resented most about Hoffman and his kind (beside the fact women were thought to best serve the revolution on their backs, when not busy serving coffee) was their exasperation with anyone who didn't subscribe to their particular set of values. Being told how to think is offensive, whether it be by radicals flogging autobiographies or art directors selling magazines. Isn't pluralism and the open market of ideas why people gravitate to a place like New York in the first place?

Like that *ur*-American rebel George Washington who pleaded with his doctors to stop bleeding him and allow death to run its course, I pray we let Abbie's surrender be the final death knell of the Decade that Refused to Die. Hedonism isn't social transformation, it's *hedonism*, just as *believing* in change is not, in itself, change. Like some bedeviled sin eaters, we have been force-fed the bread passed over the bloated corpse of the '60s for the last ten years and now it's time for us, we who came after, we of the Shadow Generation, to expel it from our system once and for all. Let. It. Go. Utopias are meant to be lost, isn't that what makes them Utopias . . . ?

**Four Calls**
September 6, 1980
8:43 P.M.
Four calls today, all upsetting in their own way.

Call 1: Mary thought she could sell me as a food stylist (of all things) on some no-budget tabletop shoot she's doing backdrops for next week. She actually was rather sheepish when I talked to her, not sure of my response, whether or not I would take it as an insult. The fact she was hesitant to even suggest it made it that much easier to decline.

I'm broke, I should be thankful she thought of me at all, yes, yes, I know. But I can't really see myself toiling over some unearthly lard mix trying to make it pass for ice cream or painting chickens with that liquid smoke goop to give them that "oven roasted" (toxic) glow. Didn't want to know what it paid. Somehow it's easier that way.

Call 2: Billy Sirk wants to hire me as his assistant on one of those Captains of Industry portfolios for *Forbes*. Wants to try to get me into the sack is more like it. Someone must have told him of my newfound singlehood and now suddenly he's there for me. American men can be so transparent, you'd think he would give me a bit of recovery time before making his bid, unless of course, and this is a far more likely scenario, he's simply looking for a quick fix.

"I know you're not ready for a relationship, neither am I. Soo . . . I thought maybe we could have some casual, non-committal sex until we are . . ." One offer I think I can resist.

Never understood why people use assistants anyway. I'm insecure enough about my technical skills, the last thing I need is someone looking over my shoulder, silently second-guessing my every choice.

Call 3: Yet another job offer, this one from "Ric . . . without the 'k,' " some friend of Marvin's who has a "wake-up" service. Fifty bucks a day and all I would have to do is show up at some basement apartment in Chelsea every morning from six until ten and in my most soothing, sex-kitten voice purr into the phone, "Good morning, Mr. _____. It's time to get up." Six in the morning? He offered to give me *my own* wake-up call but I told him I didn't think it was practical—my phone is usually unplugged at that hour.

Call 4: Mary again. She has a wedding next month and wants to hire me to shoot it as her gift. Ingenious idea but do I really have to be a part of this, I mean I can say no, can't I?

I hate shooting weddings (Does that sound as bad as I think it does?), particularly ones as froufrou fussy as this one is bound to be (St. Patrick's ceremony, reception at the Carlyle). So much import and consequence coerced into a single day.

And if and when the marriage ends in divorce, all that remains of the union (aside from the kids of course), the only hard evidence these two people were ever together, is the wedding album, that perfectly preserved Rosetta Stone from the day mommy and daddy promised they would never do what they have now done.

Was it all dress up and pretend, the kids wonder, this wedding, just make-believe for a day? They seemed so happy in these pictures, before they had us. . . .

Given the choice, I think most photogs would agree with me. David Bailey once bragged he'd only done two weddings in his life—one for a neighbor when he was still a teen and didn't know better and the other for the dreaded Kray twins who presumably made it clear saying "no" was not an option, no matter how polite the regret.

From my perch, the whole proposition known as marriage plays like little more than an improvisation on a sinking ship where, at the first sign of rough waters, there's a phalanx of lawyers and therapists ready to guide you and your brokenhearted kids straight onto the rocks of misery. Not too long ago I saw a preview for a new Natalie Wood movie whose title says it all: *The Last Married Couple in America*. Even Hollywood gets it. Need I say more . . . ?

On a more positive note, I hear tell that Condé is toying with the idea of reviving *Vanity Fair*. New hope for the wretched?

## My New Book

September 8, 1980

11:17 A.M.

Marvin just called to wish me a happy birthday. Wasn't going to mention it here but I guess the date gives it away—twenty-eight. Last year I threw a red pepper at B in frustration over having hit twenty-seven. Can only wonder what kind of godless act I may commit tonight. Martyr and Farter (B's names for Mom and Dad, self-explanatory I think) are on the Queen again so I suspect I'll be fielding a two-minute ship-to-shore special before the day is out. Would prefer a check of course but pride, lofty pride would never allow me to cash it, even if it were in the mail.

Marvin's pressing me to do a book. Again. Claims to know someone at Aperture who is quite keen to take a look at anything we may want to put together. Marvin, of course, has volunteered his services as "creative consultant," whatever the hell that means.

I can't quite figure out the motive behind these periodic pushes of his. It's not like he needs the gig—he just finished the *Esquire* redesign, for god's sake. When I confront him as to why he is so anxious for me to do a book, he demures. Then, in a small but firm voice tells me he just wants to share my "genius"—that's the word he always uses, "genius"—with the rest of world.

Why is it when someone praises my work I immediately distrust not only their opinion but the integrity of the work itself, as if approval is not the proper response? Not that I can take a compliment, I can't, never could, but that's not the point. He doesn't understand why I would rather keep my work for me . . . at least for the time being. A book to me still seems too arbitrary, there are too many elements at play that have nothing to do with the photograph. The pictures are bound (and gagged) then suffocated between two covers, ready to begin their slow-bleed into lifelessness. (God, I can turn dramatic when depressed!)

My guess is he wants to try and attach my name to a monograph, then appoint himself my dealer, although he hasn't actually come out and said as much. Of all the horses to ride. If I ever *do* have call for an art pimp, though, I could certainly do much worse. Pity I'm not attracted to him. We are friends and always will be but just that, *friends*. And may I never give cause to allow him to stray from this description, no matter how "convincing" his ministrations.

On the other hand, what better way to get a gallery to give you a show than by slapping them with a coffee-table book, that gloriously useless testament to having arrived. It's so bass-ackwards it just might work. It is lovely to be wanted, and I'm sure I'd miss the adoration should he suddenly decide to play mentor to a younger, firmer budding talent, but it does get rather confounding at times, this mixing of the personal with the professional.

### 2:00 P.M. . . . After Some Errands

Just invited Marvin to come over and raise a glass to yet another year of *moi*. Might go through the Fat Girls with him if I can work up the gumption. Some of the stuff I like—particularly of the dying deer. The blood registers as shadow in b&w—very fortuitous choice to go with the Tri-X. It occurs that maybe what Marvin wants in the end is to increase his profile amongst the SoHo-on-the-make set by positioning himself as some kind of art-world Svengali to the pliant and anxious. "All the better to fuck newly-minted MFAs with my dear," I can hear him cooing.

Does everything revolve around sex or is that just *my* current fixation? Am still too hot and bothered to sort that one out. Would that I only had an object for my affections although I'm not sure "affections" is entirely accurate—"compulsion" might be closer to the sensation I'm feeling. I suppose if I'm still feeling this desperate in a month-and-a-half I could always get myself fucked silly at Plato's—Dirty Uncle Lech says they're reopening for Halloween. A fleshy fright night with (not so) perfect strangers anyone? And to think I have ten more years before reaching my sexual peak . . . I'm going to explode first, with no one around to pick up the pieces.

## Zipless Fucks

September 9, 1980
9:14 A.M.

Marvin surprised me last night with a camera bag (Domke) for my birthday. A sweet man to be sure, but also terribly shrewd. He's now taken to calling my technique "posed candids." I think I prefer "hit-and-run," sounds less pretentious, more action-oriented. Besides, if photographers do indeed steal the soul, isn't it wise to run as fast as your little feet will take you before your subject can ask for it back?

Marvin always acts incredulous at how people seem to open up to my camera so readily. As if there was some grand secret I was keeping to myself. Maybe the secret is I shoot only the "unfamous," the ones who have nothing to protect or perpetuate. Or perhaps people just trust a woman with a camera more than they do a man, particularly when she's as anonymous (read: plain) as me. Besides, women are natural portrait takers, we *get* it in a way men don't.

Ironically enough, it always feels very sexual to me, the question of who to shoot. Obviously, any portrait begins and ends with the face. But it's also the demeanor of a subject that attracts, the way they comport themselves, their choice of clothing and how it sits on their body. The trick, for me at least, is to try and capture my initial sensation on film before there's too much conversation and who they think they are, i.e., the subject's own self-image, begins to assert itself.

The camera between us makes it easier to keep the words to a minimum—the focus stays on the task. I want nothing from them but their likeness, their image, the way they appear at that particular click of the shutter, and for their part, they usually want nothing more from me than to be done with it. When it works, it's printed, fixed, and pushpinned front and center onto my wall. There it stays for my perusal until, ever so slowly, it gets inched toward a corner and eventually into a drawer, replaced by a newer fascination.

The whole process can and often does amount to little more than a no-risk, fantasy version of a pickup. Very clean, very safe, no Goodbar/Gere freak-out scenes. Jong's "zipless fuck" mediated by a lens. Why can't it be so easy in real life? (More importantly, Why must this always be a rhetorical question? she asked in solipsistic obliviousness.)

I think Marvin liked the Fat Girls contacts I showed him but he's almost certain D. Arbus did something similar in the late '60s. Don't know if this means I'm on the right track, hopelessly derivative, or merely that it's all been done before. Maybe . . . I'm on the right track *and* hopelessly derivative *but* it doesn't matter precisely because it *has* all been done before. *Someone* please advise.

## Still Dead
September 10, 1980
6:35 P.M.

In light of the other night's revelation thought it best I get myself to the Arbus show that's up at Robert Miller ASAP. One series is street candids, the other Coney Island, both pre-'65. Very consistent stylistically with her later work if not as distinct. Collectors don't seem to mind though—almost half the show was sold before it opened, at up to $6,000 per. Why is it dead rebels and living conformists are the only artists who sell?

Most of the signature techniques are there: the straight-on confrontation of the subject, the blanching of the skin tones, the enigmatic visages. That woman was nothing if not a stalker, a Great White Hunter, the perfect picture of the Other her bounty. Marvin claims to have seen her working more than once around town, and, apparently, the intensity on her face when shooting was so severe you thought she was either in pain or about to lose her mind.

With stakes that high I can't help but think it was inevitable one day the hunter would be captured by the game. As career moves go, it doesn't get much better than suicide to ensure an inflated market for your work, but had Arbus chosen to live we almost certainly would have been spared shows like this.

I'm not sure why her daughters would OK such an exhibition beyond the (mis)perceived need to keep mom's name alive and/or cash in on photography's newfound viability as an art form, a.k.a. investment. This show will sell out not necessarily on the strength of the images themselves, but, because of the simple fact it is all that's available—these clearly inferior pictures are, in effect, elevated by the resonance her published work continues to have. One does, however, have to wonder if the estate ever stopped to consider there was a *reason* she was so sparing with what she put out there for public perusal.

Arbus only released work she knew to be "indelible," images we couldn't forget. Something she seemed to understand implicitly was that the more mediocre images there are floating about in the ether, the harder it is to make memorable ones. Once the Godardian nightmare kicks in and we're all walking around with palm-sized video cameras dangling from our necks like some great battery-operated albatross, what then? The world as one, interminable home movie?

If art is an argument, Arbus was more persuasive than most. She took things to the unequivocal precipice, declared that to be the center, and never bothered to check her back. I have to believe she signed out when she did not because she had lost her sanity but because she had said all she had to say, and saw no point in reiteration. There are many days when I think I am perfectly capable of doing exactly the same should I ever find myself having reached a similar plateau.

When artists hit upon something that finds a collecting public there is always the pressure to churn out endless variations of that initial success. Mozart often complained of being paid to repeat himself. Duchamp gave up art (or so he claimed) for library science and chess. Arbus not only gave up art, she gave up on the world or at least her place in it. Where else was there for her to go with work that extreme?

While she may have successfully avoided the pitfalls of careering, the same can't be said for her executors. If, like for most artists, your work is tantamount to your *life's* work, posthumous missteps by those you've entrusted with your reputation—your own flesh and blood in many cases— surely is a fate worse than well, death. And Arbus isn't alone. There's a long tradition of deep-sixed disgruntleds. Just ask Papa Hemingway how he's feeling toward *his* brood right about now.

### Joey and the Shark

September 11, 1980

11:55 P.M.

Just in from the Shark, a place I should never go alone. And not just because of all the Tony Benedetto and Frank Sinatra on the juke. Tonight, however, the walls in here were beginning to close in, making me crazier than I already was. Had to get out. Sense-memory made me take the right onto Spring and before I could grasp what was about to happen, there it was—the Shark.

Should preface all this with the fact the mailbox held a horrid little surprise for me this afternoon when I got back from Doc Vermin's with Kertesz—a letter for B addressed in a woman's hand and doused, literally *sodden* with perfume. How it evaded Tom the Mailman's yellow forwarding stamp, and why this particular letter had to be the one to slip through the screening process, kept me going around in my head for hours.

Tempted, was very tempted to open it until I finally resolved it wasn't worth the personal indignity, choosing instead to conjure up possible profiles of its doubtlessly purple-prosed author, using my highly evolved sense of smell as a point of departure. While the New York postmark wasn't making it any easier, I decided it was probably from one of the following:

A.) An ex from London, recently touched down on this side of the pond and finally feeling brave (desperate?) enough to get in touch.

B.) An actress from one of B's endless series of acting classes, back from L.A. and an ill-fated sit-com season. Hadn't yet been given the word he had a "roommate."

C.) One of those Upper Eastside Ladies Who Lunch whose apartments he used to always be doing work on . . . among other things, I'm sure.

Rather stunning how little prompting it takes to set myself back. Which I suppose is the "challenge" with having to consciously kill someone off in your mind: it's not really something you can train yourself into or even work at. But what in the world are you supposed to *do* exactly while building that numbing distance between you and those blessed little memories?

Swore to myself never to go in the Shark again after the night that Guido in the white loafers followed me home and "serenaded" me from the street. Had Mary picked up her damn phone and/or had I not promised Grampa that I would never drink alone ("An anti-social corruption of what should be a social pursuit," he claimed, to which I now say, "EXACTLY!"), all this would be moot.

The minute I sat down, something felt terribly amiss and then I realized; no Joey. In all the times I had either been in or by the Shark, Joey was always the guy behind the bar. The day guy—there was a persistent rumor of one, I just never had actually seen him—was on tonight, but why, I still don't know.

This much I *do* know. Vicente was there, my wannabe goomba suitor, and even he was giving me the runaround.

"Where's Joey?"

"Joey's not here."

"Joey's *always* here."

"Joey's gone away."

"Away where?"

"Stand up for me . . . turn around in a circle. How come you still wearing pants?"

This was about the usual routine, his way of ignoring whatever it was I wanted to talk about and commandeering the conversation back to what he wanted to talk about: our, at least in *his* mind, imminent date.

"Is he sick?"

"You wanna go out with me you're gonna have to put a dress on. Men wear pants, girls wear dresses."

"Vicente, I can't go out with you—you're married."

"Why you say that?"

"Why is there a tan line on your ring finger?" He examines the fingers of his left hand as if seeing them for the first time.

"That? That ain't nuthin' but a little eczema."

There's a pause as both of us finish our drinks and regroup.

"I've never been in here when Joey wasn't serving."

"I told you, forget about Joey. You say his name again and certain people are going to come over here and they're not going to be looking to buy you a drink. Capish . . . ? Now stand up . . ."

And back-and-forth it went. A few drinks later, my courage up, I try to steer the conversation back to Joey again at which point Vicente surreptitiously squeezes my wrist so tight he leaves a mark. It was beginning to feel like the set of *Mean Streets*—if only Johnny Boy would appear, ridiculous hat and all, and turn this place upside down. Then we'd get some straight answers!

They say Little Italy is the safest place to live in all of New York—it's a close-knit community where people take care of their own. They also, unfortunately, have been known to *eat* their own. A Darwinian survival technique used to keep the tribe strong, I suppose.

Joey, I gather, was no stranger to certain less than above-board pursuits, numbers-running being the most oft mentioned. Now whether he took the wrong guy's money or what I can't say. But Jimmy Hoffa, he was not.

Hopefully, he'll be back where he belongs tomorrow. I can't even consider the alternatives.

### The Music of Our Lives
September 12, 1980
12:05 P.M.
Elton John in the park tomorrow. For free. How else would they get people to come? *Goodbye* Yellow Brick Road, already.

We're still waiting for you to make good on your promise, Reg, still waiting for you to take your boas and high-heeled sneakers and your funny glasses and get the hell back to that farm you keep going on about.

Ahhh, the music of our lives. The Peace and Pollutions get Jimi and Janis to claim as theirs and theirs alone while we Shadows are expected to make a meal of the Eltons and Eagles of the world. And when a band that actually has something to *say* rather than exists simply to sell records finally *does* manage to break through, they always seem to implode.

Case in point: Joy Division. They're about to start their first tour of the States and what does the singer do? Hangs himself over a beam in his bedroom. I guess when you name your band after the Nazi "endearment" for the death-camp women they used at will, there's bound to be some complications on the road to mass consumption.

A friend of Marvin's from San Francisco told him Byrne and Eno are out there making a record collaging "found sound" from the radio, stuff like short-wave exorcisms and Middle-Eastern singing. Yes, please.


## Chelsea Death Trip
September 13, 1980
9:49 A.M.
It's rare that a stranger invites me out and more uncommon still when that stranger sports a Mohawk. Was out walking

Kertesz yesterday in Little Italy (still no sign of Joey), when one of New York's Lost Boys, all limbs and gaunt cheeks, knelt down and placed a flyer at my feet before skulking off. It announced that something called the Plasmatics (Punk? New Wave? No Wave? Can't keep up!) were promising to blow up a Cadillac on a Chelsea pier come dusk. My presence was kindly requested.

Not one to shy away from mindless spectacle, I arrived at the appointed hour to find a healthy number of office worker/functionaire-types mixing uneasily with the obligatory chains-and-leather set. The suits were looking to kick off their weekend with a few cheap thrills before retreating back across the river, while those still confusing nihilism with a lifestyle choice had emerged *en masse* from their Lower Eastside squats and panhandling stations not only to bear witness but presumably participate in what was being billed as this generation's answer to Happenings.

The assembled knew the potential for wanton ruin when they smelled it and the firetruck and ambulance parked judiciously at the head of the pier beside the intended victim—a fiery red Coupe de Ville literally wired to the roof with explosives—only fueled the bloodlust.

At the opposite end, by water's edge, was a makeshift, saturnine stage, covered funereally in various flower arrangements and RIP placards. The whole thing looked more like a movie set than a concert, with multicolored cables spindling off in all directions around cameras and light towers. The sheer dollar amount expended in the name of glorified demolition lent the scene a certain air of decadence extreme even for Manhattan. If what we were about to indulge in was to be just one more form of cheap, escapist entertainment, at least ravaging a symbol as fecund as *the* American luxury automobile (a nicely twisted paean to King Elvis perhaps?) would go a long way in justifying any guilty pleasure. Or so I was trying to tell myself as I snapped away at the crowd, waiting for the band to come on.

Looking rather flash in white tux and tails, the guitarist eventually appears, churning out a three-chord din and then a girl, looking more dominatrix than singer, commences to screech about God knows what. A song or two later (it was difficult to discern just where one song ended and the next began), she and her personal cameraman start down the length of a police barricade to where the Caddy and the real fun awaited.

The band thrashes it up another notch, as the woman introduces the car to the ways of the sledgehammer. Only after every window has been relieved of its glass, does a technician start the thing up and send it barreling down the pier toward the stage.

The band plays on, safely dispersed to the sides, as the Caddy plows its way through the Marshall stacks and over the edge of the pier. At the height of a vaulting, graceful arc they set-off the dynamite, neatly separating roof from car and sending both hurling into the squalid Hudson below. The more fevered of the crowd stomp and howl for an encore while the rest are too busy tussling over metal scraps to worry about "more." (What more could they possibly have come up with . . . detonating the pier?) A rather large, private security detail quickly clears us out and the mini-concert/movie shoot is over as quickly as it began.

Overall, a very revealing display given the band's shameless pandering and its fans' "as scripted" Pavlovian response. There is something refreshingly bold about a group that asks nothing more of itself than a bit of the old ultra-violence. Some of the Punk bands seemed to have been moving along similar lines of inspiration but never had the inclination (let alone cash) to choreograph such impulses so formally. *Spontaneous* rather than orchestrated combustion seemed more the tenor of *that* time.

The evening serves as yet another reminder that a surprisingly large cross-section of the population, a critical mass even, will buy into just about anything as long as it is done *in extremis*. And make no mistake about it—sustaining such nothingness *has* to be much harder than it looks.

Packaged, prefab nihilism delivered as post-adolescent rebellion and available for replay over and over again—clever, that! All an evening like this proves is how difficult it has become to be genuinely transgressive and maybe even, forgive me for thinking this but . . . how *irrelevant* transgression is now. Seven or eight years ago the idea of my going to an Alice Cooper concert used to scare the shit out of Martyr and

Farter. Now Mr. Alice is playing golf and having cocktails with M and F's friends in Greenwich. *Plus ça change* . . .

## Thirteen
September 17, 1980
7:07 P.M.

Seem to be on a teen kick lately, particularly teenage girls, vestiges of the Montgomery Ward catalogue job last spring, no doubt. Not quite sure just where the fascination lies, surely am *not* looking to recapture my lost (read: squandered) youth let alone be reminded of how quickly whatever comeliness I might still have is beginning to fade, but teens and teen girls in particular no longer seem to be allowed their simple awkwardness. It's never too early to start thinking sexy, seductive, hot! With the Fat Girls I was trying to get at the fallout such a mentality creates—what it's like to be made to feel uncomfortable in your own skin at such an early age.

Saw something yesterday that struck me as a corollary. Buying my usual passel of papers at my favorite Yemenite newsstand, I noticed on the back cover of *Backstage* a cattle call for an Edward Albee adaptation of *Lolita*. Nabokov's been dead all of what, three years? and already they're picking over his bones for inspiration.

Called Jacobs, who passed, claiming he didn't think it was "quite right" for the *Post*. A room full of jailbait strutting their stuff in front of a couple of fat-cat producers? If they think that doesn't fall within the parameters of the territory

Murdoch has staked out for himself then maybe they need to start reading their own paper.

Should early teenhood seem a bit young to be displaying your pudenda on stage, you wouldn't have known it from the turnout. By the time I arrive, the line of (mostly) mothers and daughters has already snaked out of the conference room and into the hotel lobby. Almost to the one, the adults are nervously grasping their child's headshot while the youngsters feign indifference, when not surreptitiously trying to suss out the competition.

Once inside the audition area I can see Albee himself is conducting the interviews. A producer-type sits slightly behind him to whom Albee periodically defers. The ad warned those over thirteen need not apply but judging from what I see no one is taking the producers at their word. Fifteen-year-olds giggle when asked their age, barely able to contain their glee at lying to an adult while their parents look on in silent approval. A pair of high school seniors play it straighter, not wanting to draw too much attention to themselves. I think I may even spy a couple of recent college grads, done up in pigtails and sun dresses, so intent on landing that first paying gig they can't fathom just how deluded their decision to audition appears to the outside eye.

The high point of absurdity comes when one backstage mother, irate over an Albee question, snatches her daughter's headshot away from the producer and cries: "Of course she hasn't read the book, she's only sixteen!" before grabbing her child's hand and storming out in high dudgeon.

Didn't see any of the usual stringers lurking about the lobby but was told somebody from *People* was due later. Nabakov and *People* magazine—there's an uneasy union. Whatever would a displaced Russian aristo possibly have made of what passes for culture in this country? No wonder he spent so much time with the butterflies once he got to Cornell.

Should New York ultimately prove bereft of the perfect fetching young thing, might I suggest the producers take their prepube star search to Paris and seek out that Humbert manqué, Roman Polanski. Surely *he* knows a nymphet he'd be willing to serve up in the name of Art.

Got home in time to see on the news that the Sandinistas finally got Samoza, bazookaed his bulletproof Mercedes somewhere in South America (Paraguay?) straight to oblivion. Left a crater the size of the Sea of Tranquility. All in all not a bad day.

## Bergman, the Towers and Me
September 18, 1980
8:45 A.M.

I'm somewhere sun drenched, a resort, maybe on the Med, and it's hot, unbearably so. I'm hiding in my room basting myself in drinks with little umbrellas in them, waiting for things to cool OFF. It's a very unnerving experience because I know there's this splendid sea just on the other side of the door but I'm too delicate and pampered to leave my climate-controlled room.

So I'm alone (again, naturally) and beginning to wither from the booze when there's a knock on the door. It's room service with yet another drink, only this time it's a different waiter, someone I recognize but can't quite place.

He introduces himself as Ingmar Bergman, and he's right, he *is* Ingmar Bergman but why is Ingmar Bergman bringing me my umbrella drink? Because, he replies very matter-of-factly, he's come to take me back with him to the more temperate climes of Stockholm where he is about to teach a master class at the Royal Swedish Academy.

I've never acted in my life. Why me, Ingmar? He assures that beneath my veneer of complacency there's a thespian tigress waiting to be unleashed. More to the point, I bear an uncanny resemblance to the muse/love of his life, Liv Ulman—with whom he has recently split—and whose absence has made it impossible for him to work. Only I can reanimate him back to his old creative self—the future of the Bergman oeuvre hangs on my decision.

Well, far be it from me to question the casting prowess of Ingmar Bergman! I'm about to pull my suitcases from the closet and start packing when B (who else) appears, wedging himself between Ingmar and me on the bed.

"Stockholm," he declares, "is out of the question!" I am the woman who is going to bear his children and no child of his is going to be raised by an actress.

(Given his virulent anti-thespian stance here, he must have been doing more construction work than acting which, when you think of it, was true in real life too, except of course when it came to our relationship.)

I'm embarrassed by his grandstanding in front of the master and tell him so. It's too late, it's over, I'm going to Stockholm. But haven't I seen the paper? The picture of B jumping off the roof of the World Trade Center with the marriage proposal written across his parachute? I'm laughing so hard at this point I'm left with no choice but to wake up.

Simple politesse should dictate that dreams are interesting only to the dreamer and possibly also their therapist, who is paid for the inconvenience of having to listen to them, but if I, shrinkless and alone, can't commit my dreams to paper, in the privacy of my own notebook, what's to become of such nocturnal emissions?

Yet another reason I so loved B. (Please note tense.) He actually encouraged me—it sounds so ridiculous now—to *share* my dreams. Lying in our morning bed, his warm hands caressing my stomach, I could sputter on endlessly about whatever it was that had me laughing and/or muttering the night before without fear of ridicule or reproach.

God, how I loved those hands, the discolored fingernails and the permanent calluses. They were the hands of a working man, very different from the patrician palms of those who came before him. Aside from his smell, it's those hands that I (will) miss the most.

But I digress . . .

I only bother to include this dream because for once I can trace where it came from, at least the parachuting part. A couple of days ago, a guy who could have been B's doppelgänger actually parachuted off one of the World Trade Center towers while his girlfriend below photographed him coming down. If that ain't love.

How I made the leap (sorry) to marriage and Bergman well, isn't that what keeps psychiatrists in pipe tobacco and all but the most inner-resourceful (or prideful) laid out across a couch?

## Cocksucker Blues Redux
September 19, 1980
8:02 P.M.

The *Post* finally made good on their promise of work, calling yesterday to see if I would cover the opening of the Robert Frank retrospective at the Whitney. Robert "The Americans" fucking Frank?? The man who blew out every conventional notion of photography way back in what, the '50s? The first one to make me see that a picture could indeed be something other than mere re/presentation? Fuck the art speak, this is the guy who came up with the cover for *Exile on Main Street*(!), for Christ's sake!!!

I was surprised someone like Frank would hold the interest of editors as unapologetically lowbrow as those at the *Post*, until they told me the museum was screening *Cocksucker Blues*, Frank's handheld, behind-the-scenes travelogue of the Stones's '72 American tour/debauchery, a film purportedly so raw and unforgiving, the band themselves, Lucifer's own, demanded the thing be buried.

Failing to suppress it outright, lawyers for the Stones reached an agreement with the filmmaker which, if I remember correctly, prevents Frank from showing it for anything other than "educational purposes" and even then it can only be screened a certain number of times a year. (Who says the businessmen aren't sucking the life out of rock 'n' roll??? And people *still* don't know why the Sex Pistols had to implode.)

The Whitney has been very much in the news this week, having just been the first to break the million dollar mark for the work of a living artist, a Jasper Johns American flag of all things. As controversial as that purchase may have been (Is it a flag? Is it a painting of a flag? Is it worth a million clams?), it pales in comparison to last night's events.

It wasn't particularly surprising who turned up. Reheated sixties-vets (if not outright survivors) and their tie-dyed-in-the-wool, next-generation understudies (most of whom's last museum experience must have been when their mother led them through the dinosaur rooms at the Museum of Natural History) were kept waiting outside, while a steady stream of Junior Committee Young Heavies were whisked into the cocktail reception preceding what had been billed (no doubt for contractual reasons) as a public screening.

What *was* surprising was the sheer number of people expecting to get in. New York's "great unwashed" had been camping out since the night before, with the line snaking up Madison, across 76th Street and ending at the far side of Park. Tarpaulin Town had plopped itself firmly in the craw of America's most desirable zipcode and there was nothing the Ladies Who Lunch and their rainmaker husbands could do about it.

The scene could have been grafted directly from the old Fillmore/Schaeffer Fest "rock" (love that word) days: the open pot smoking, the requisite playing of "dress up" (a smattering of Edwardians though most were sporting the studied "anti-costume" costume of bells and tees, with Fryes for the men, Birkenstocks for the ladies), the great forests of hair . . .

Nobody wants to grow up, least of all myself, just as no one believes Mick *won't* be singing "Satisfaction" at forty but how old do you have to be before recreational drugging and promiscuity without end becomes, can we say, embarrassing? I'm beginning to sound like a disaffected parent here, ironic given the age of most of them.

No one, it seemed, was expecting this kind of turnout, least of all the museum. I'd been there a half-hour and they still weren't opening the doors to the public. Instead, guards were in deep conference, reviewing the finer points of crowd control, while administrators debated how to gently break it to the faithful that seating was at this point "limited," if not altogether nonexistent. A dicey proposition at best, for however into the crunchy, live-and-let-live nature of things folks like this may *profess* to be, they still have a great deal of trouble taking "no" for an answer, as in, "Sorry, but *no*, there are *no* more tickets."

When the word finally does come down that the film has indeed begun without them and they should all come back tomorrow to try again, the reaction is predictable, at least to those of us familiar with the sensibility that informs the shaggy beast of rockdom. The small group of guards at the entrance is soon overwhelmed by some of the more vocal in the group, who then run interference for a flood of frustrated followers up the staircase to the theater.

A tug-of-war begins over the theater doors with another set of guards who are holding their own, prompting someone to yell, "Other side!" which sends the great unwashed roaring through the Hopper exhibition to the unguarded exit back by the phone booths, and voilà, the screening is now, as advertised, open(ed) to the public.

Those inside first appear bemused by the late arrivals, as if it's all part of some Living Theater performance piece. That notion is soon torpedoed when the invaders start overturning chairs, none of them empty. By the time the screen is separated from its ballast, Junior Committee members are polishing war stories for the cocktail hour of how, with great cunning and assurance, they somehow managed to fight their way out of the darkened chaos to live another day and tell the story of the great (white) Whitney riots.

Needless to say, Jacob and friends at the *Post* were ecstatic over the debacle, patting each other on the back for having had the good sense to cover it, even going so far as to compliment me on my "moxie." Very newsroomy turn of phrase I thought, very *Front Page*. Little Miss Moxie . . . that's me, front and center. Now how about a retainer for Miss Moxie, eh fellas?

### Here Today, Gone Later Today
September 21, 1980
10:46 A.M.

Have been laying very low lately, as my silenced phone will attest. All it takes is not returning a call or two and shazam, your name goes to the bottom of the deck and won't come up again unless someone needs something. Well, maybe that's not *entirely* true.

Practical New Yorkers (and New Yorkers are nothing if not *practical*, which to the outside eye could conceivably be seen as Machiavellian) have two sets of friends: those they call "New York" friends and those who actually *are* friends.

"Friends" you give the benefit of the doubt and likewise you expect them to weather almost any slight *you* might inflict. You want them in your life because no one else is quite like them. New York friends, conversely, are by definition inter-changeable. A New York friendship has at its very foundation the tacit understanding that we are all on secret final warning. One fuck-up and you're out—the city is much too wide-open, too filled with other possibilities to have to bother with forgiveness.

There are no second chances because there is and always will be something bigger, better, faster out there to replace you, if not in truth, then at least in theory. This is, in case you've forgotten, *New York*. As long as you understand the way the game is played you won't get hurt, but from the outside it must seem somewhat, can we say, bloodless?

Having said that, not even my *friend* friends seem particularly anxious for an update on little me, maybe because they know there is none. Could it be I've exhausted my sympathy quotient with endless tales of B woe (sounds like a Shanghai noodle factory)? The fact that I haven't exactly been keeping up with *their* lives couldn't also be a factor, could it . . . ????

Change, flux—they seem the only constants these days. Don't get too attached to anyone/thing, for it will all be over tomorrow. Not *could* be, as they say about one's life, but *will* be. Whether it's relationships or neighborhoods there's a constant churning that goes on here, an endless turnover of faces and façades.

A premium placed so squarely on the New means memory is necessarily short, with all eyes directed squarely toward the future, the eternal tomorrow. Very hyper-American. We destroy our architectural heritage (the old Penn Stations, Met Opera House, countless pre-wars) and replace it with pale, thoroughly modern imitations, which, we assume, prima facie, are better for no reason other than the fact they're New. History, one might deduce, is for losers.

With its bedrock of granite and opportunism, *New* York has always been in the business of rebuilding itself. One swing of the wrecking ball and the past, with all its failures and shortcomings, is replaced with something shiny, optimistic—something New. The rub is we're becoming better known for what we destroy than what we build, no matter how much dirt may fly.

Romances here can cut along similar paths, which must be why half the city lives alone. An endless stream of possible new companions, compounded by a severe lack of faith in any kind of permanence, leaves many settling for serial, sequential relationships. Commit and switch. Here today, gone later today. Cityscape and its effect on the psychology of those who live in it—how's that for the power of the rational mind?

**Dread**
September 22, 1980
9:23 A.M.
Bob Marley collapsed in Central Park yesterday. He was jogging with his band, on the way to Sheep's Meadow, looking for a pickup game of soccer. In the middle of another world

tour, two SRO shows at the Garden, and he simply fell down and couldn't get up.

Rumors are swirling: the CIA had him poisoned to keep him from backing Manley and the Socialists, Rita messed with his food to put an end to his womanizing, cancer . . . Almighty dread!

'80

FALL

## A. A. (Artists Anonymous)

September 24, 1980

3:45 A.M.

Just in from another one of Lech's patented night crawls through what they used to call the demimonde. This one ended with a pagan celebration marking the equinox, an ushering in of the new season. Thirty of us sitting in a circle on an Avenue B roof, acting out a very funny script rife with Bacchanalian ritual.

Getting there was half the fun. A junkie on the corner of B and 5th saw us looking for building numbers, thought we were going to cop and wanted in. Once we finally convinced him we weren't there for the drugs, his only reaction was to take off his belt and threaten to wrap it around my neck if we didn't give him money. Lech, God bless him, quickly set him straight.

"Remember: never bring a knife to a gunfight," Lech chided after wrestling the belt away and throwing it up on the fire escape above us.

"My wife gave me that, you bastard," the guy protested, holding up his pants while staring longingly at the belt dangling down, just out of reach.

"Lucky for him, he still *has* a wife," chuckled Lech, as we slipped into the open door of the building. Lucky for *me*,

I didn't bring my camera, I thought, as we made our way up the crumbling stairs to the roof where the party was roaring.

We kept toasting up there until there was nothing left to lift, at which point a woman across from us starts blubbering on about how no one understands how hard it is to be creative in this town, how she can't go on, etc., etc. Ah, yes, the hapless life of the unknown artist. Who did she think she was talking to?

Would have had more sympathy had it not cut so close to the bone but a few minutes of this and I can no longer help myself. I lean over in Lech's direction and say sotto voce, "If she doesn't jump soon I'm going to throw her!"

Not wanting to laugh out loud Lech coughs into his beer, nearly choking. To be heard above the commotion, the girl turns more strident, until those of us who are trying not to listen no longer have a choice but to acknowledge her and her plight.

What began as a joyous gathering of primitives has now been shanghaied into some kind of disgruntled Artists Anonymous support session. (Hi! My name is Skip and I'm creative.) People are encouraging the screed, seconding her complaints, huddling around her as if it was group-grope time at an Esalen encounter session.

As cold as it may sound, what comes to mind is that not long ago this woman's protest would have been dismissed as being self-evident—why even speak of it? Which is to say, since when did being an artist become a legitimate career choice, where a graduate degree plus hard work gives the guarantee of success?

There's a pretense of entitlement ingrained in some of the newer arrivals on the scene, as if their year in the Whitney Program is the voucher that guarantees promotion up some mysterious ladder of recognition. Were they pissing and moaning about a life doomed to obscurity in the old Cedar Tavern before the academy took hold? Do I even have to answer that?

You're either an artist or you're not—it's not something that's suddenly conferred with a diploma. What happens to your work—your success or lack thereof—depends on nothing more than taste, politics, and more than a modicum of blessed good fortune imparted from the very gods whom we were toasting last night. It helps if you have talent but talent alone won't get it, ye rooftop malcontents.

The bad juju up there was about to send *me* over the ledge so I ditch Lech and head downstairs into the host's apartment. Somebody said it was the last place Charlie Parker lived before he died. It looked it.

For reasons best left unexplored, I soon follow into the bathroom this cute if somewhat dim bulb who had been ogling me earlier. Pulled him into the tub where we start kissing—probably took me for a drug whore, but it's not drugs or conversation I'm after, just some nasty, heavy tonguing-down, which we manage quite nicely, thank you, until someone starts pounding on the door and the moment is lost.

Sheepishly, we emerge. Lech is nowhere to be found which comes as some relief, not being up to any explanations. After one last cold kiss goodnight, I leave my passing fancy standing next to the fridge, ready to follow me home—no more prompting needed. What more could a girl ask for? Will answer that one once I find it.

### Children of the Rich
September 25, 1980
11:12 A.M.

Quite the afternoon yesterday, the details of which I am reluctant to include here for fear of laying bare just how craven I have become in my desires.

Fuck it, girl—Mao is dead! Throw down that little Red Book and revel in your glorious, decadent Western mind. They can't haul me off to the hoosegow for window shopping, can they?

My all-too-brief brush with male perfection began with a call a few days back from the older sister of Alexandra Bowe, a college classmate I sometimes bump into at tonier Uptown-comes-Downtown parties. While someone like Alex no doubt finds it "kicky" to slum it down here every so often, big sister probably only makes it below 14th Street when her driver's license has expired or she's shepherding her in-laws to the Statue of Liberty.

Everything about this woman screams serious money, a walking, talking incarnation of that old Anglo-Saxon saw about the upper crust being a load of crumbs held together by dough. While little sister goes out of her way to downplay her background, this one clearly revels in it. And so be it— lord knows I certainly am not one to comment on someone *else's* relationship to the lettuce. (The sensibility wrought by this life of self-imposed indigence has become so second nature, I'm not sure I'd still be able to properly adapt were my fortunes to somehow change.)

Carolyn or "Bunty" as she insisted I call her, was interested in having me photograph her teenage daughter. Nothing too formal mind you, just candids, or as she put it, "Some hanging-out shots. . . . That seems to take up the bulk of their waking hours at that age anyway, don't you think?"

Seeing no reason to alienate her so early in our conversation, I agreed. But honestly? When I was that age? "Hanging out" wouldn't fully describe how it was we spent our time. Basically, my clique lived in Central Park. More specifically, we burned a path between the bandshell, where we copped our drugs, and the woods by the boathouse where we did them. Our parents just thought we loved the outdoors. So much so that at least once a year Mother would idly float the possibility of moving to Connecticut, where I'd have real woods to play in. Marvelous vision, Mom, but where was I going to score my windowpane in Rowayton??? Besides, Dad had read enough Cheever to know he was not, nor would he ever be New Haven Line material, J. Press button-downs and Brooks ties notwithstanding.

Bunty soon started getting cold feet, fretting over how her already alienated daughter would react to someone following her around all day with a camera, someone hired by her mother. I assured her I had what it took to win over the youth of today.

After a few more Bunty pleasantries—how quickly the little bastards grow up (which I punctuated with a quote from cummings only to have her attribute it to Rod McKuen), what I've been doing since Barnyard, what her sister *hasn't* been doing since Barnyard, where we should meet for drinks to discuss the particulars, etc.—I finally offered to simply show up the following Saturday morning where we would take it from there.

That left only the fee. What was my usual day rate? Depends whether it's editorial or advertising. Which category would this fall under . . . ? Neither. I could hear her squirming on the other end, frustrated by her inability to get a range she could use to lowball me. (Is the only reason the rich have more than the rest of us that they're that much tighter?) I let her off the hook, $250 for the day plus prints. Selling myself short once again to someone I should be gouging but then the business side of this business was never my bent, which, as logic would have it, is why I never seem to have any real money.

Dickens had it right when he characterized New York as one big marketplace. This city's not about black or white, Left or Right, Uptown or Downtown—those are just canards devised to underscore our differences and keep us apart. Horizontal, "separate but equal" arguments. What matters, the *only* thing that matters is the vertical, the top and bottom of it, i.e., who's up in the penthouse drifting among the clouds and who's down on the ground floor, in the back, with the nesting pigeons. Bunty, I sense, has never had to confront the endless "coo-coo" of a nesting pigeon.

So this morning I arrive at the appointed hour, Upper Eastside in the '60s. Bunty has cadged herself a very large, meticulously preserved townhouse, a block or so from Avedon's horse stable or whatever that behemoth was before he converted it to a studio. An older black woman answers the door, dressed more like a nurse than a maid (or is it "housekeeper"?), and sends me through the Sister Parish living room and on up to the fifth floor . . . via the elevator. No point in being obscenely wealthy if you have to climb stairs.

The lift door opens and it's The Slits on the stereo, loud, nightclub loud and thumping, the deep, skankin' bass reverbing off the marble floor. Back behind the speakers, at the far end of the vastness is a swing suspended from the sixteen-foot ceiling, where sits a young man who, well, let's just say if I could build myself a plaything this creature would be it.

The whole package is very Carnaby Street-meets-Mudd Club, from the hobnailed boots on up to the pageboy haircut. Fine tawny skin, thick, brooding lips. And the eyes, really no need for conversation with eyes this dark. Only problem, he's more of a boy than a man, twenty, twenty-one in the shadows, too old to be involved with a high school senior but, *malheureusement*, too young for an ancient like me.

He immediately rises upon seeing me enter the room, turns down the music and offers me the swing. I'm so flustered that when I try to put down my bag, all my film—ten or so rolls—empties onto the floor. I scramble after them, red in the face as he holds the bag open for me.

It's beginning to feel like an Audrey Hepburn "meet cute" confection until that out-of-body thing kicks in, the one I usually get when having particularly self-conscious sex: I'm watching myself watch him and am extremely embarrassed by my open fascination but can't seem to stop.

"Are you lost . . . ? You look lost."

(O, happy day, an accent of some sort.)

"I don't think so. . . . Is Marcy here?"

His face falls and with it some of the crackle between us. I've asked the obvious next question, the one the situation requires. As far as he's concerned though, he's been snubbed. I'm not here for *him*. Oh, but how the fragile male ego never fails to amuse when it's not busy angering!

I want to let him know I could give a shit about Marcy, that I'd much prefer standing right here, dipping into those deep browns but it's a much needed payday that's brought me here so maybe, for now at least, it's best to simply follow the protocol.

We introduce ourselves. The boy's name is Robert. Corsican, not French as I had thought; a thought I thankfully kept to myself as the one thing Corsicans detest more than the French are those who mistake them for French. Reminds me of my first roommate after college—a Corsican—who constantly blurred the line between his end of our railroad hovel and mine, a problem I finally solved by playing *chanson français* records at full tilt. Anything by Brel, Piaf, or Aznavour (his Unholy Trinity), turned up to eleven seemed to do the job. It may have cost me my woofers but not before it drove him around the bend and into another apartment.

"Marcy's in the greenhouse . . . behind you."

I turn to see a truncated set of stairs and follow him up. At the top is an open, loft-like space, bigger than most Manhattan apartments, awash in mid-morning light streaming down through a vaunted skylight. Very *Klute*-esque. Monsieur Bob makes the introductions. Marcy, partially hidden amongst rows of ferns and exotic palms, is watering what appears to be a sinsemilla plant. She looks up just long enough to acknowledge me, trying hard to portray bored, which should come easier to a chick with a swing and greenhouse in her bedroom. Either way, the "Hello, I'm in the room" hair betrays her pretense.

I decide to let her be aloof while I gather myself, fumbling through my bag trying to choose a lens, a relatively simple task were it not for the presence of the Boy. He is my only focal point, everything else—the shoot, the sad little rich girl hiding behind her ferns, this hothouse of a rumpus room—it's all been reduced to static on the distant periphery in his presence. Something very stirring about him, the way he seems so comfortable with himself, at ease in his own skin, how he looks you in the eye and is very direct, warm without pretense or attitude.

I start worrying that maybe I'm being obvious, maybe I'm giving myself away too soon. For her part, Marcy is growing increasingly impatient with my presence, finally dropping her watering bucket with a thud as if to announce (through the leaves) that while she may have no choice but to cooperate with me, she would like to get it over with as quickly as possible. The Boy takes this as his cue, whispers "good luck" to me, and disappears back down the stairs.

A long, unnerving silence ensues, which I use to assemble my camera and take some light readings before she finally emerges from behind her flora. Not knowing how long she'll last, I try and mix it up, ever aware of the capricious attention span that curses teendom. I start her in her garden, move her down to the swing and then, once I know she's eased into being the center of attention, convince her we should try some things in the park. By this point I hear the elevator kick in, taking with it, alas, Monsieur. Jesus wept.

She's a *jolie laide*, this girl, her face an odd amalgam of exaggerated features and acute angles. Beneath the insecurity that comes with being a gawky teen though, there's a feral self-possession that girls her age aren't supposed to have quite yet mastered. If I'm going to deliver a picture that can sit atop the family piano or side table long after she's left the nest, something suitors when brought home for the first time can use as silent confirmation they've made the right choice, it's that self-possession which needs to come through.

We'll see—won't get the contacts back until the end of the week. Truth be told . . . ? I'm much more interested in her boyfriend. Ghosts of B, take note.

## Remy Time
September 27, 1980
10:32 P.M.

On the way home from the lab tonight I saw a street poster announcing a call for entrants to a show that's going up next month in the waiting room of Grand Central. Remy Martin—"an inspiration to artists for over two hundred and fifty years"—is the sponsor, and they're offering a bottle of their best to those selected.

They work hard to kill us with indifference, then those that don't succumb they try and buy out with a bottle of cognac. Who said it doesn't pay to be an artist in this town? Made me think of that poor girl on the roof the other night—she sees this poster and we really could have a jumper on our hands. Poor her. Poor me. Pour us (anything but) a Remy.

### Thin White Duke Does Great White Way
September 28, 1980
11:45 PM

After not being able to pry *Scary Monsters* from the turntable for an entire week, I decided to take myself out tonight and scalped a ducat (where *is* that press pass?!!) to see the "Bowied One" open on Broadway as the Elephant Man.

A rock 'n' roll suicide bleeding down the Great White Way it was not. Thin White Dukey Boy actually surprised, gamely contorting his still lithe body into convincing approximations of physical deformity while delivering his lines in a staccato ("I . . . am not . . . an animal . . .") that was enough to make you forget Philip Anglim.

The pre-show scene outside the theater was Big Fun, so much so I couldn't stop hammering away at myself for not bringing a camera. The tuxedoed set looked lost amongst the swell of leather as the t-shirt bootleggers and scalpers lurked in the shadows, surreptitiously displaying their goods while checking their backs for cops, who, anticipating the unruly crush were mounted on horseback for the occasion.

When John Belushi arrived, not on a horse but on foot (lost his limo?) and alone, the place positively erupted. He signed autographs and riffed away to anyone who would listen until the flickering lights called us to our seats. How long before that guy makes his Broadway debut? Is there a house big enough to hold him?

As for Bowie, he really did acquit himself quite nicely by

anyone's standards, with the possible exception presumably of Frank Rich. Dressed in nothing but a Gandhi diaper, he's not exactly what you could call beefcake but if you go for that pallid, sunken chest, English-school-boy-run-amuck look (yes, please), the night goes that much faster. The irony of us all coming out to drink in a near-naked rock star playing a freak in much the same way Victorians must have laid their two bits down at the sideshow to gawk at the real John Merrick could not have been lost on the producers. Little matter, the run is all but sold out.

To put Bowie on Broadway is a coup. The rock concert is now less about the ritual of a shared experience, less a Shaker dance of collective ecstasy and more, much more, about the cult of personality. Just to touch the hem of his diaper, as it were. The more intimate the setting of the communion, the more transcendent the experience. In other words, it's seeing Bowie so up close and personal more than his actual performance that sets the kids to lighting matches and screaming for curtain calls.

It must be painfully obvious to those trained in the theater what's happening here. Why should producers hire a mere actor when they can get a "personality"? Why limit yourself to an aging Broadway audience when you can tap into the far larger fan base of a pop god like Bowie? Rock fans these days will follow their stars wherever those stars choose to take them, be it the colossal (football stadiums) or the barn-like (hockey arenas). Bringing Bowie to Broadway is just another way of exploiting that "star" power and at much higher prices than you'd pay to see him at the Garden.

What W. Burroughs predicted twenty years ago is finally coming home to roost—the "Algebra of Need" I think he called it—where both the consumer and the product they're consuming become hopelessly simplified and degraded over time. To wit: Next month the Dead are supposedly doing a Halloween run at Radio City *and* selling tickets to a simultaneous broadcast of the shows fifteen blocks south at the Felt Forum. Kids standing in line overnight, waiting to buy tickets to watch Jerry Garcia nod out on a giant TV screen.

Bowie on Broadway is just a variation on that theme. Whether the guy can actually act or not is almost beside the point. If he can (*The Man Who Fell to Earth*), it's considered a windfall, if he can't (*Just a Gigolo*), well, hey, whadya expect? He's not an actor, he's a *rock star*. P.T. Barnum phone home, all is forgiven!

### Old Man's Darling

September 29, 1980

7:45 P.M.

Back from a day out on Montauk with Marvin. Glorious there today, more like Indian summer than early fall. Have no idea why I agreed to let him take me in the first place, must be getting lonely. I think he senses as much and wants to be around in case I should have a momentary lapse in judgment.

I won't. Though I might have come up with a workable idea for a photo essay: the demise of the drive-in movie. Passed an old abandoned theater on the way out, looking very forsaken with its cracked marquee and weeds pushing up through the concrete floorbed. The introduction of Daylight Savings Time suddenly made the late show too late for most people, I guess. A small price to pay to help keep the farmers in the fields, but still. Made me almost nostalgic for *Billy Jack*, the only movie I think I ever saw at a drive-in. (Lake Winnipesaukee, 1971?)

Usually I don't like to leave the city if I don't have to but being by the ocean seemed to agree with me today. Marvin claims it's because our bodies consist of 99 percent water—it's where we feel most at rest. Says JFK used to remind the press of that fact every time he abandoned Washington for one of Papa Joe's seaside getaways. If the options came down to spending summer either in a city built on a swamp or at the compound in Hyannis . . . is an explanation even needed? You're the president for god's sakes!

It was certainly a generous gesture on the part of Marvin to take me away for the day but still can't help wondering what the catch is, if not sex. (And when it comes to what animates men into acts of generosity, what if *not* the promise of sex?) Maybe he just likes my company, surprise, surprise. Better to be an old man's darling than a young man's slave, right? Are you listening, B?

## Pablo Picasso Is Not an Asshole

September 30, 1980

6:04 P.M.

Today was, as most in the city seemed to realize, the last day of the Picasso show at MOMA. Have been putting it off—all the hype made it that much easier to delay—until the eleventh hour when it became an impossible ticket.

Should anyone doubt PP's having been cast as the preeminent artist of the twentieth century, five minutes on 54th Street this afternoon surely would have set them straight: scalpers demanding 50 bucks and getting it (not from me, of course, not after my Bowie extravagance), self-starter types with duffel bags peddling t-shirts bearing the master's signature. The ticketless faithful were becoming progressively more frenzied as the afternoon wound down—reminiscent of the bedlam of the Stones movie at the Whitney the other night. Not bad for someone who never bothered to cross the Atlantic, let alone learned to play guitar (although he painted a few).

Knocked off a roll in less than twenty minutes, much to the consternation of the bootleggers, until I bought one of their tees, of course.

This isn't the first time the American public has stood in long lines outside a museum. Mona Lisa apparently drew unprecedented numbers to the Met back in the early '60s but she has close to three hundred years on Pablo. King Tut a few years back must have broken some records, but the man was a King and a well-preserved one at that. Besides, most probably came to ogle his gold—gold can have that effect on people.

Safe to say that with this Picasso show art, "Art" with a capital "A," has officially entered the arena of popular entertainment. And if an exhibition like this can now be perceived by a critical mass as a must-see event, a "blockbuster" à la Tut or *Star Wars*, then Picasso, to put it in Warholese, is Art's first undisputed "superstar."

Cultural shift or a testament to one guy's star-power? Either way, it's now clear to me why he had so many wives and mistresses—if his pull is this strong from the grave, imagine what it must have been like when he was still able to get it up.

The guy at the front desk said the museum estimates over a million served, a number I must admit I'm still having trouble swallowing. The cynic in me says the majority of those attending did so more to be part of the legend-making than out of any genuine appreciation for the work. They come for the *event*, to mingle with the myth of the "modern" artist we're told Picasso so perfectly embodied—that irascible profligate who fucks who he wants when he wants, paying for it all with an endless font of work that springs from him with preternatural ease.

Motivations aside, what can't be denied is that for the first time we've inducted an artist into the popular iconography—anointment by t-shirt, if you will.

"Pablo Picasso never got called an asshole . . . not in New York," sez The Modern Lovers.

"You know it," sez I.

## I Vant to Be Alone

October 1, 1980

11:32 A.M.

Personal stereos—"walkmans" is what the Japanese are calling them—they are everywhere, or so it seems, now that I was almost killed thanks to one. "Walkpeople," these people who walk around wearing their stereos on their heads, they may do their walking *among* us but they are definitely (and defiantly) not *with* us. Once the unit is attached to the belt and the headphones are in place you have pretty much put the rest of the world on visual notice that you are to be left to your own modulated privacy. Expand your personal space and take leave of it at the same time—a very cynical response to an all-too cynical city.

Perhaps this is the white boy's way of combating the ghetto blasters that keep coming down from parts north, a kind of reactionary crawling back into the self as if to say "fuck off" to you and the soundtrack of your life that you seem to have no compunction about foisting on the rest of us. My life has its own soundtrack, mofo, and guess what? I'm keeping my soundtrack for myself because *I* have nothing to prove. Ouch!

The death of boogie box machismo, not a bad idea. And one day there won't be graffiti on the subways either. In the meantime, I should start buying stock in Duracell.

## A Girl, Her Dog and Sensible Shoes

October 2, 1980

7:12 P.M.

Friends are beginning to call again, the word must be slowly seeping out that I've been coming up for air. Am kind of surprised, particularly after I completely shut most of them out to be with B. When the conversation comes around to the particulars (and it always comes around to the particulars), I simply tell them that like all poorly understood episodes in my life, I don't really want to talk about it.

Some back down immediately and change the subject, but there are those who press on, offering how I should have seen it coming, how the man was no stranger to betrayal, that he did, after all, leave someone else for me, etc., all of which only leads me to agree that love is nothing more than that extra effort we make with those we really don't like anyway.

Which is precisely why I don't want to talk about it. Since being thrown back into the pond, I'm getting the sense women are holding their mates' hands just a little bit tighter when in my presence. Curious how marked the division between the coupled and the uncoupled. Attached tend to run with attached as if mingling with the freelancers will lead straight to "wife swapping."

(Such a quaint, relic of a phrase: "wife swapping." Wonder if Gay Talese ever came across the phenomenon in all his years of "field research" for *Thy Neighbor's Wife*. How many women does a married man need to screw before he's qualified to write about infidelity anyway?)

Suffice it to say, the world to me now feels like one giant, ongoing game of musical chairs where the music has stopped and I'm caught without a place to sit. But as cold as it might seem out here in the Land of The Forever Standing, the upside is there's no one left to please. I'm letting my hair grow, all over. No more waxing the nipples or the "trail of happiness" that starts at my navel and runs due south. No more fretting over the fuzz on the nape of my neck or the small of my back. I've decided to let my body return to its natural state of repose. Take me as I am or don't take me at all.

Thank goodness for the distraction of the streets, one of the few simple pleasures New York still affords someone as woeful as me. It's that occasional inadvertent meeting of eyes that not only keeps morale up but also helps explain why most of us have such an overactive fantasy life. As a woman you learn reflexively how to deflect, to turn aside the male gaze without incident, but we *all* look as we move through our day, women and men, photographers and non-photographers alike.

I always think of Whitman and his cavorts through these "passionate and mettlesome" streets, continually sizing up potential lovers with that insatiable longing of his. A walk here is pure urban safari, the idle hunt for something to titillate the (mind's) eye in a rough of passing humanity. It's an endless display rife with potential and it's that *potential*, the "what if," that we all thrive on.

Men are easy enough, given the proper motivation, so I guess I'm not worried. But there is that sense, particularly when out walking Kertesz, that something may have gone terribly wrong here. I mean, a brokenhearted gal dutifully walking her loyal dog leaves me just a pair of sensible shoes shy of premature spinsterhood. Should I be worried?

## Narcissus to the Pool
October 3, 1980
9:21 A.M.

Mine is a neighborhood in "transition," as the real-estate leeches will be only too happy to tell you, and now that it's getting easier down here to find brunch than a hardware store, the good people at Manhattan Cable have finally gotten around to wiring the block. SoHo, my little corner at least, has at long last joined the realm of the "demographically desirable."

The initial impulse behind my signing on was to get rid of the ghosts, not the ex (if only), but those distracting double images. While that little black box may improve reception, even increase channel choices, it can't do a damn thing about the quality of the programming. Mediocrity has always been what TV delivers best. Now, with cable, I just get more of it.

Was beginning to take it personally until recently when I stumbled over Channel J on the Public Access band late one night. Public Access takes a kind of Mickey Rooney/Judy

Garland approach ("Let's put on a show/My dad's got a garage.") where absolutely *anyone* can spout off in front of a camera on a first-come, first-served basis. (Democracy works—Politburo, take note!)

There's a very fine line between guileless amateurism and outright exhibitionism and these "shows" go a long way in blurring that edge. Like Narcissus to the pool, every over-inflated ego and/or whack job in the five boroughs capable of scraping together the $25 air fee can crawl out from under their rock and air their most lurid obsessions. And air them they do. If it sounds good on paper, it's even better in the flesh, flesh being the operative word here, at least with Channel J.

*Interludes After Midnight* has as its tag "the first nude talk show" which pretty much lets you in on what you're going to get—something I always appreciate when it comes to my porn—and what you get is two very hirsute, very corpulent men, one with mic (the host), one without (the Ed McMahon character), sitting bare-assed on what appears to be a wrestling mat in the middle of an empty, windowless room.

After a brief, gratuitous discussion on current events (presumably the "talk" part of the "talk show"), an aspiring actress, more often drugged-up than not, joins our two Lotharios on the mat. A casting-couch moment, without the benefits of a couch. The groping session that invariably ensues gives new meaning to the concept of a talent show, a kind of Arthur Godfrey unbound.

Once the men have established what their aspirant won't allow, they segue into what she will. This then serves as the foreplay part of the audition. The three soon reconfigure themselves into a human sandwich, with the men taking the role of the bread and the actress the meat. Our host "Daniel Jay" (not, I think it's safe to assume, his real name) then takes some time to plug one of his upcoming adult films, after which it's back to the mat for another audition.

Along similar lines, *The Ugly George Hour of Truth, Sex, and Violence* has his Ugliness (someone who for once lives up to his moniker) coursing Midtown streets in a gold metallic sweat suit with an unruly video rig strapped to his back, looking for women who will give him a shot at convincing them to show us their breasts . . . and whatever else they might have. He is our sweaty "professor," we, his "students." His running commentary ("Arch your back . . . are you listening, students?") vigilantly instructing us on the finer points of persuasion and breast photoplay.

Heaven knows I appreciate the female form as much as anyone, but the real pleasure here is watching his Ugliness doggedly pursue and cajole. Like the professor himself, we the viewer have no idea where the next willing victim will come from. Much as in "real life," the thrill is in *la chase.* Whether or not his quarry ultimately accedes is never quite as entertaining as that initial reaction and negotiation.

Those that grant George his request usually do so with qualifiers. Most need to get off the street first, which is catnip to our host as it gives him a chance to talk them into his Williamsburg flat—the "Polish Penthouse"—and, presumably, out of their pants. For others, the back alley offers a sufficient level of comfort, while the real gamers simply pull up their shirt on the spot, only too happy to share their twins with the late-night cable crowd. It's as if all we had to do was ask.

Would love to do something on these guys for the *Post*. Now that they're about to cancel David Letterman (just as well, no one needs to be watching TV in the morning), they're the only two shows I can't stand to miss. Jacobs would feign indignation that I, for a moment, would think they'd be interested in such smut. They're too busy imploring Ali not to go through with his upcoming fight. It's been front page, what, four days running now? Must be hard after being told you're the greatest all those years to now hear it's time to say good-bye. I can't say *who* exactly is supposed to tell the champ it's over, but somehow I don't think he wants to hear it screamed at him from a tabloid.

The landlord's wife came around today looking for B, wondering who I was, what I was doing in his loft, etc.—the usual routine. It was all I could do to keep from telling her I'm the one whose check she cashes every month but saw no point in provocation. The old lady (or, more to the point, her son) smells gold in these them hills and would love to get me out, I'm sure. One more thing (not) to worry about.

## The American Handshake

October 5, 1980

11:00 A.M.

Yes, it's eleven in the morning and I'm still drunk from last night. May have even had sex, in fact I'm almost sure of it, not that it was forgettable, but I was so wrecked I can't really be certain.

The old Fillmore East, that one-time citadel of hippiedom, has just reopened as a gay dance club. The guy who owns St. Marks Baths has pumped something like $3 1/2 million into the place. "The Saint," like the designer jean, is For Members Only . . . for $150 a year. Apparently the rumors of disco's death have been greatly exaggerated—there's a two-year waiting list.

Went up there last night hoping I'd unearth some fantastic slice of subculture to dangle in front of Jacobs but became quickly convinced I had sent myself on a fool's errand. The door was a fortress of bouncers surrounded by leather boy/lumberjack clones vying for entry, and then there was me, standing in the middle of the slough, a woman scorned.

Finally, I manage to get the attention of a Keeper of the Gate who informs me there is simply nothing he can do. My press credentials are irrelevant, he explains, for unlike the rest of Manhattan's nightlife fiefdoms, The Saint, dear girl (with an emphasis on *girl*), isn't run by "publicity whores." How refreshing!

Having run out of ears, I decide to simply invoke my quasi-Fourth Estate prerogative and let *myself* in. I'm fumbling my way toward the stanchions with their sacrosanct purple velvet ropes when there, just inside the door, stands everyone's favorite Corsican.

A frisson of expectation swells inside, like something positive could actually be about to happen here, something portentous. Then it occurs, abruptly and oh, so cruelly: the guy must be gay. Of course, how could I have missed it? How could someone so fine *not* have that deep narcissistic, same-sex, make-love-to-yourself fascination?

Unwilling to give up on the vision *that* easily, I jumpcut to a different scenario: he's straight, he just *works* here. He's an inducement, a blandishment, eye candy, a paid variation on the shirtless muscle boys they put behind the bars at Studio 54. The worst-case scenario I'm able to stomach is he's some kind of rent boy, a hunk-for-hire, arm charm, an escort to some heavily closeted power broker who doesn't have time for relationships so he buys them. A trick yes, but a trick who, given his druthers, prefers the fairer sex.

My internal story conference is interrupted when the object of my conjecture turns around and looks directly at me, or rather *through* me. I'm waving, holding up my camera, yet he doesn't register who I am until I call his name. I explain the situation, he has a word with Clipboard Man and chop chop; the rope comes down, the sea of malcontents parts and it's time to kiss the boys good-bye. I. Am. In! Who *has* this guy fucked?

The music is thunderous, so loud there's no point in trying to converse. The Boy signals me to follow him, but there is such a crush of people we're soon separated. No matter, there's enough here to keep me busy for a while.

There are two, maybe three levels—hard to tell with the light show-cum-planetarium projections—all tarted up to look like the interior of a space rocket. We're in the mothership, a giant womb with body parts flailing everywhere: arms in arms, hands on crotches, tongues in mouths, everyone in various states of undress and ecstasy.

They're all done up in jockstraps and jackboots, tight jeans and bandannas, holding poppers under each other's noses, moving and sweating in one giant throb of hedonistic rapture. The place has a hardcore devotion to pleasure and freedom that reminds me of Paradise Garage in the early days only without the "gay lib" context . . . but who needs context with a clusterfuck this good?

Something else is unusual about this place, something I can't quite articulate until it dawns on me no one is drinking. Juice bar—no booze. The place is completely dry, a little spit of semi-sobriety in the heart of cross-addicted downtown.

Twenty minutes later I finally find the Boy in a corner chat-up. He says his quick good-byes then takes me by the arm (Love it when they do that!) and leads me through a side door into a Checker that sends us streaking down Broadway. I have film to process and tell him as much. He has other ideas.

"You can do your work later, no? We should go to the beach."

"Isn't it a little late for the beach?"

"Not this beach—I will show you."

He moves over to my side of the cab, makes himself comfortable. Don't want to tell this guy no, (not yet at least) but I'm not prepared to give up on Jacobs and the *Post* yet either. He tells me he understands, and doesn't look as disappointed as I would have hoped.

Through my high school drool I soon hear myself backpedaling, throwing my paparazzi future to the Fates.

"Alright, we can go. But only if I can ask you a question."

"Of course . . ."

"What were you doing in a club like that. I mean, odd place isn't it to bump into a guy who runs around with Chapin girls?"

He laughs uncomfortably, sensing my "disorientation."

"I am not gay if that's what you mean. And if it is Marcy you are worried about you have no reason. She is a child."

A relief, I must confess. On both counts.

"Me, I prefer a more mature woman . . ." he relays, leaning in with those big browns, ". . . like you."

"Mature . . . ?" Is this boy too young to realize that's not the word a woman who still fancies herself a girl wants to hear at a time like this?

I'm trying, really trying, to ignore his innocence (or is it insolence?) as he directs the cabbie down to Battery Park and a fenced-off area by the river called Art Beach. (Demerits to me for never having bothered to check it out, god knows Kertesz and I have been by there countless times.) The gate is locked but he knows a spot where we can squeeze under the fence.

We're settling into the sand, watching the moonlight refract off the Twin Towers, when he pulls out a bottle of scotch he's been carrying around in his Danish schoolbag. Very strong but very, very good—the perfect social lubricant.

At water's edge there's an installation, a string of full-length mirrors coming out of the sand, reflecting Jersey back to itself. Standing in front of one, arms around each other, we look like quite the couple I think, or at least we look *like* a couple, age difference be damned.

There's a wooden slide where we make out for awhile before he tries to take it further and I have to ease his hand away.

"Sorry . . . but my uninvited guest has arrived."

He looks more confused than crestfallen.

"My period . . . I'm menstruating . . . bloody mess."

"Ohhh . . . I don't mind."

"I do."

And even if I didn't, we were going to do it in a bed, the first time at least. He must have agreed because the next thing I remember is trying to find a cab. The only other thing moving over there at that hour was rough trade drifting down from the Christopher Street piers, so we were left no choice but to stumble back to his place on Walker(?), somewhere just below Canal at any rate.

Once in the space, I remember being stunned by its rawness and the sight of an ungainly motorcycle hanging from a pair of rotting I-beams. Can't be sure just what did or didn't follow but this much I do know: when I woke up, my watch was gone (the plastic Japanese one, thank god), but more to the point, I was naked. Checked myself for stains, oil or otherwise (he's hung the motorcycle directly over the bed), then set about looking for my clothes which I eventually found neatly placed on an old museum display case housing a collection of perfectly dissected frogs.

And it didn't stop there. At the far end of this place, between a series of floor-to-ceiling windows, there was a casket suspended between two pediments. Peculiar enough but I can deal, I thought, until I realize a body is inside . . . and it's not moving.

Screamed bloody murder and instead of waking the dead (or Monsieur Bob for that matter), I awaken his roommate who very matter-of-factly steps out of the casket-cum-bed and introduces himself. Had I not been in quite such a stupor, I'm sure his nakedness alone would have been enough to send me running out of that place right then and there. Flying Harleys(?) (not that I'd know a Harley if it fell on me), sliced amphibians, caskets for beds . . . am I missing something here?

Wish I could remember if we did it or not. Think I may have given him a blow job, B's "American Handshake"—yes, we Yank girls *are* easy—and promptly passed out. Ask me no questions, I'll tell you no lies.

## Nice Girls Do!

October 6, 1980

10:12 A.M.

Every time I let myself feel even a *soupçon* of elation over the other night's adventure, I realize anyone I might try and share it with would probably see it as nothing more than a tawdry encounter, excusable only in light of a certain someone's having left. I've never really understood this: am I supposed to feel guilty for sleeping with a guy on the first night? Or for enjoying it? The act of sex has had over a billion years to evolve, surely we've reached the point where we no longer have to worry about such things. Isn't that what the pill was about, giving women the prerogative to act like a man???

This country has always been threatened by female sexuality, which should tell the unenlightened just how potent a woman's carnality can be. Potent or not, sex still seems somehow absurd to me, all that fumbling and animal heat as an expression of what . . . love? I mean, do people really fall in love, storybook style, as if they don't have a choice in the matter? Or is it all simply a function of need and proximity, learning to tolerate another's peculiarities long enough to form some kind of bond that will then keep you in each other's orbit long enough to procreate and perpetuate the species?

Sometimes it feels like I could fall in love with just about anyone provided a certain number of basic criteria were met, fidelity not necessarily being one of them, which makes me very French if not exactly Corsican. I must say I do quite like Monsieur Bob, even though I think it best just to forget him. Now that someone has actually presented himself, I can see it's too soon after B to do anything about it. It's probably more about the desire for *desire*, what I'm feeling now. And besides, he's too young to do anything else but nothing, i.e., forget him.

Tired of thinking about it. Chemistry will win out over analysis every time, at least when you're as hungover as this. I didn't give him my number, did I?

## Black Night
October 7, 1980
10:59 P.M.

Mary is in the hospital, and they won't let me see her until tomorrow at the earliest. Was busy brooding about the young Corsican, wishing he'd call, wondering why he hadn't called, wondering if he'd *ever* call, when, mercy me, the phone actually goes off. The voice is in paroxysms, sobbing fragments that are hard to put together.

"It's Mary . . . she's hurt . . ."

"Leon?"

"She's hurt . . ."

"She's hurt what . . . ?"

"She's hurt . . . herself . . . over us. . . ."

It was Leon, the man I assumed and very much hoped I would never have occasion to speak with again. Leon, the filthy professor who ran up coed body counts like it was a perk of the teaching trade, all with a sense of entitlement rare even amongst the most hardened of academic predators. Leon, the lapsed husband wailing over the very same woman he had only recently traded in for a newer, firmer design.

"What happened?"

"I don't know."

"Where are you?"

"St.Vincent's . . ."

"I'm coming . . ."

"They won't let you . . ."

"Has her mother been . . ."

"She's coming . . . it's not my fault, M. L., you have to believe me . . ."

How's this going to look to the outside world? How, Leon! I was able to eventually get it out of him that Mary had immersed herself in a warm bath before taking a knife to her wrists, which is where the cleaning woman found her semi-conscious and about to drown.

According to Leon she was going off to Woodstock with some guy she met last week, and, when he canceled last minute, this was her response. On a dazzling fall afternoon, she sinks so low she quite nearly disappears. Can't shake the fact that had I stuck to our original plan and gone with her up there, she may never have drawn that bath. All because I felt topped off on her and *her* little tale of woe.

As much as I distrust Leon's motives, his preoccupation with his own culpability, I must admit my reaction isn't much better. Mary wanted kids, he didn't. The marriage soured long ago, no one's been happy for years, and so Leon rides the first train out that will have him. *Someone* had to make a move.

Once she gets over the sting of rejection, she'll realize Leon is one less asshole in her life. In the interim, she goes from a self-assured, semi-successful artist to a "Stepford Wife" who can only define herself through a husband who's never been there for her. A painter with a gallery that actually sells her work, who has stopped painting because a bad marriage is finally over??? I mean, I *want* to be sympathetic . . .

If this is her idea of a cry for help, I'm afraid it may have backfired. She's in the hospital licking her wounds, Leon's busy doing damage control on his own hide, and the rest of us are left to teeter between guilt and wondering why the breakup didn't come earlier. On *her* terms.

She's only thirty-three, there's still time for children *and* with the right guy. Women like Mary (and myself, if I am being honest) are the first to trounce others for their spinelessness, yet the minute everything's not perfect in our own lives we collapse. *Our Bodies, Ourselves*, alright, OK, but then what? "Do me" feminism where anything short of that is considered masochistic?

Is this quagmire we've been floundering about in simply fallout from so much ovarian consciousness raising or something that cuts deeper, something we're all susceptible to regardless of whether we shave our armpits or not? I'm certainly not holding any keys here (could you tell?), but it seems we have bought into our own polemic to the point where we're no longer sure how to be both independent *and* part of a loving couple. I'm beginning to think men aren't the only ones confused by the Women's Movement.

As for you, dear Mary, may you rest easy tonight.

## Black Night Part II

Reeling from Mary and my own inability to cope, I took my camera out on one of those late-night crawls, the kind that invariably leaves you bleary-eyed and pinched in some "greezy" spoon watching the sun rise over runny eggs and soggy toast.

Trying to sleep was, once again, impossible. The loft was too dark. I felt like a cave dweller without a torch, one eye opened and waiting for the dreaded saber tooth to pounce. When I sat up in bed watching what I took to be the couple in the opposite loft fucking, only to realize many minutes later it was the billowing of curtains, I knew I had to get out.

Someone's been doing these great—what to call them, hieroglyphics?—in white chalk on the blank black paper that gets slapped up over expired ads in the subway stations. They have their own iconography—a barking dog, radioactive baby, stick figures—rendered in a visual shorthand that's stunning in its simplicity and self-contained grammar. Strung together, the images form a kind of sentence, the exact meaning of which is elusive, and that's what attracts me.

Apparently I'm not the only one. People are stealing them almost as fast as the artist does them, which is why I thought I should try and document them in their natural habitat before the MTA catches on and shuts down the whole show.

Coming up from Spring on the 6, I spy one at Astor; a barking dog and astronaut floating freely across the "black hole" of the poster paper. I get off a few snaps when two skinheads—jack boots, suspenders pulling their jeans up over their massive, corn-fed, suburban-runaway stomachs— approach from behind, wondering aloud what it was I thought I was doing.

Ignoring them was the first mistake, turning my back the last. One jumps me while the other takes to pulling at the camera. Your first reaction is disbelief. This. Is. Not. Happening! I ask in as sweet a voice as I can manage to please let go, but it's clear they're not interested in what I might have to say so I pull back on the camera with all my weight and scream. My shriek must have tipped them off as to the extent of my attachment to my livelihood, and they decide to settle for my bag, the one Marvin just gave me.

They're running for the exit, and I'm yelling to the token clerk, who's finally ventured out of his kiosk only to watch, stupefied, as the skins continue over the turnstiles to the other end of the platform, down onto the tracks and into the tunnel, last seen headed uptown. If they were that hell-bent they should have said something. Token Guy had never seen such brazenness, which made me feel better, until he pointed out my eye was beginning to swell.

Time for a drink, but the droogs now had my cash and cards. (Naturally, the plastic was maxed out months ago.) Bradley's was the nearest place I could think of where I might see someone I knew (Lech?) at that hour so I head over to

University. By now it's 1:30, the last set of the night's just beginning. Major Holly's doing his grunting duet with his bass, someone's gently having at P. Desmond's piano, musicians are drifting in from their gigs earlier in the evening looking to unwind. The barkeep is new to me but says he knows Lech—is there a bartender that doesn't(?)—and that he hasn't been in. Too embarrassed to explain why it is I'm sitting at his bar not ordering, the guy saves me the trouble by asking about my eye, the explication of which prompts one on the house. I'm liking him already. Severely.

The gin hits my stomach, my head stops throbbing, and the eye goes numb, which is about when Lech enters, sparing me the indignity of having to try and cadge the quick follow-up demanded by the juniper berry. Lech is his usual solicitous self, outraged and effusive, insisting we hunt down the bastards who did this to me. A couple of drinks later, his fervor for justice has cooled, as has the jam on stage. Definitely time to go.

By this late hour, the transition from Lech to Letch is usually complete. The overtures begin as if cued—his wife's in Poland, what better time to finally show me his Sinatra collection? It has been a long night and I want to go home but Lech won't let it go, countering with what to his fevered brain probably seems a compromise—go check out a new S&M club with him somewhere over off West Street, take some pics, and *then* go to his place.

I'm all for keeping hope alive, but I usually know if I have any interest in sleeping with a man within the first half hour of meeting him. Why Lech should think something might still happen between us after all this time is another mystery of the male species even they can't fathom, I suspect. I would, no doubt, suffocate under such corpulence.

The guy's an adventurer, a true creature of the night who has often led me into the darker, less-traveled reaches of Manhattan Isle and for that I will be forever grateful. This was, however, one crossing he was going to have to make without me. Convincing *him* of that was another issue. Lech is a shark, and sharks can't stop moving lest they die, which leaves the rest of us who need our sleep in an untenable position.

Too sapped to argue, I soon find myself in his Mustang, top down, riding ripshod over the bloodstained cobblestone of the meat-packing district, looking for this fucking club.

The streets are empty save for a few straggling chicks w/dicks clashing with a more traditional streetwalker over end-of-night turf. When we finally see someone disappear through an unmarked door, it's proof enough for Lech we've arrived, and we rush to follow the guy in before the door is relocked, forgetting my camera in the process.

A circular set of stairs leads us to a severely underlit basement, half-heartedly done up like an Italian grotto. Judging from the looks of the rather intimidating cashier, I'm fearing we're about to enter one of those fisting clubs Lech's been going on about. He talks us past the guy, but we're then approached by a second gent who asks if we'll be needing a locker this evening/morning. I politely tell him, "Not tonight, thank you," take Lech by the hand, and we casually slip into the front room, most of which is taken up by a giant *Story-of-O* rack.

It's on this rack where you and your limbs can be stretched to that singular point where pain neurologically manages to reconfigure itself into pleasure. Having never fully grasped the inner machinations of the S&M principle, I don't pretend to understand just where or how that transformation takes place, and, frankly, I'm not yet prepared to crack that nut, not tonight at least.

The action, if that is indeed what we can call it, is concentrated not at the rack but in the lounge area. At the center of the bar sits a woman turned out in what most of us would recognize as classic evening wear for this sort of thing: leather corset with holes cut out for her twins, which are pierced and connected by a thin gold chain that she periodically tugs at, bringing them to a full, if somewhat lopsided attention.

Men line the perimeter of the room, sitting on graduated, carpeted risers in various states of undress. One is in nothing but his socks, which are held up by the kind of garters Grampa used to wear, giving him the air of an Ivy League truck driver. Our favorite, we decide, is off in the far corner shrouded in a black mask with a zipper for a mouth—the would-be Mexican wrestling star. All a place like this succeeds in doing is make me thankful I don't have to sublimate my more base urges into some disaffected, subterranean subculture—as if the isolation endemic to big city living isn't soul killing enough.

As Lech likes to reiterate, the fun in going to these "perv palaces" is not in the spectacle itself, but rather in creating the personal histories, occupations, obsessions, etc., of the habitués. It's character study for him, synopsis/synapses prompts. For a novelist—which he purports to be, though I have never actually *read* anything he's written—going to such places is like going to the gym. Mental calisthenics, locker optional.

Things begin to sour when I enter what I was told by the towel boy is the ladies' room. There were toilets of a sort in there, yes, though not of porcelain. A series of men lay prostrate across the floor, presumably waiting for me to squat over their mouths and eliminate. Somehow, the need was no longer quite so pressing.

Lech's response to my near-brush with water sport was to prattle on about the "mysterious specificity of the individual" or some such quasi-profundity. It was late so he's excused, but, the hour notwithstanding, it sounded cribbed to me, something memorized years ago to be trotted out to becalm wide-eyed naïves threatening to make their Final Exit from his circle of depravity.

It was time to go. Outside, the sun was threatening to come up, and I was very much on the crash. Lech agrees to drive me home but only after showing me one last thing, quickly. It's close and if I don't see it now, it might not be there the next time. It was something I wouldn't soon forget—I would just have to trust him. Again.

Looking for the car I could feel my curiosity fighting through the fatigue, dragging with it a second wind. His enthusiasm for this place, whatever it was, had piqued my interest, as he knew it would; and if I didn't go I would be doomed to end the night lying awake in bed, wondering what the hell I'd missed. So, once more we were off, weaving down the Westside Highway to one of those abandoned piers somewhere around Canal.

A steady stream of men were fording across the rotting pier to enter more a caricature of a building than an actual edifice, something that must have been condemned about the time Manhattan's shipping life went south. Walls were crumbling when not missing altogether, beams and electrical wiring jutted out through swooning ceilings. Five floors of ravaged infrastructure laid bare. Real Dresden-on-the-Hudson.

Shafts of new-morning light flooding down through the gaps in the roof gilded the decay with a strange glow of post-Apocalyptic calm, a living reconciliation with entropy. Time as recaster rather than common defiler. It was only after taking in the magnitude of the transformation that my eyes could then adjust to the foreground, to the specifics, the ongoing parade of men wandering like somnambulists about the perimeters of each floor. In the corners, partially obscured, knelt other men, plunged deep in chiaroscuro, waiting to take them in their mouths.

From station to station the walkers circulated, staying just short of orgasm before moving on to the next corner for more of the same. No one spoke, there was no need—

conversation would have only complicated what could not have been more elemental. The silence and its anonymity reinforced the pure physicality of the act. Valhalla for most men I'm sure, regardless of proclivity.

Lech had delivered as promised: A unique, isolated moment in time which would last only as long as the Fates allowed the building to stand or until the cops got wind and sealed it off. As such, as an ephemeral artifact of New York subculture, it needed to be recorded, and as honestly as possible.

Any hope I harbored of my presence being tolerated was purely a function of the late hour and my own particular brand of self-delusion. The open sex and my fascination with it made me little more than a Peeping Tom. To get it right without tipping over the natural order would require making myself utterly invisible, a shadow with a camera.

Rather then seek higher ground and shoot down, I stayed at ground level and slinked behind what could still pass as a wall. Crouched like a poacher inside a duck blind, I'd periodically step out, squeeze off a frame or two then recede back behind the wall and wait out any fallout. The silence in a place so massive can be overwhelming. One participant kept scanning the room for the source of that unmistakable whir coming from my Nikon. Although it didn't seem distracting enough to alter the cadence of his thrusting, I did resolve to hock my future for the Teutonic hush of a Leica just as soon as I can afford the downpayment.

My assignment completed, I find Lech waiting for me on a railroad tie at river's edge and brusquely start him toward the car. Taking no chances, I'm about to slip him the film when we're accosted by a guy in a jarhead's buzzcut and one of those close-cropped chin straps for a beard. He's buff, pumped, and about to burst out of his Levis over my audacity.

"You should be ashamed of yourself. Ashamed!"

Before I can offer an explanation, Chin Strap is waving his hands in my face, going for the camera.

"Give it. You are going to give me that film! This is something very special and very private and I am not going to let you violate *it* and our community with your damn camera!"

This guy is not just aggressive, he's obnoxious, ranting on about how my pictures will lead directly to the pier being torn down, everyone thrown in jail, blah-blah, rah-rah, woof-woof. To listen to him, the entire future of New York's gay scene is hanging in the balance over my thirty-six frames. Al Pacino and *Cruising* apparently have nothing on me!

After Lech manages to insinuate himself between the two of us, I ever so gently try to assuage the man's fear by telling him the truth.

"I shot just the building, no faces . . . !"

Chin Strap's not buying and lurches for the camera instead. Frustrated by my "bodyguard," he takes a swing at us with his knapsack, the wrong move, as it awakens the choleric bull in Lech who grabs him by the wife-beater and lifts him up into his face.

"Listen, my friend. *You* are the one who should be ashamed. This woman is a student of architecture who is out taking pictures for a class. No one is here to break up your party."

The guy looks at us both, still not sure whether to believe what he's just heard. No matter—he's not getting the film. Flinging his pack back over his shoulder in a final huff of resignation, he flits off in disgust.

Lech, my great protector, the man who will go so far as to even lie on my behalf. Too bad there's no chemistry there . . . have I established that already?

A very black night to be sure yet still somehow deeply satisfying. Feeling alone and alienated in the Big City comes as second nature readily enough but it can be just as easy to feel exhilarated by it all. Last night was a bit of both.

### Lennon in the Skies
October 9, 1980
10:31 A.M.

One of those sleepy, disconnected mornings I used to suffer through when I still thought I could kick caffeine. Eye is better but tender, still hurts to put camera up to it. Tried to make selects on the poor-little-rich-girl, based not on what I knew they'd like but what I liked. I liked nothing, naturally, save for a few frames in the park.

A mistake to use the arc light in her garden. It haloed her head, and, as much as her parents might like to think so, an angel this girl is not. It's always so hard to recognize what I was going after when I use lights, they somehow manage to wash out the initial impulse. It's available light alone from here on in, unless, of course, I motivate and start taking the time to experiment with pushing the film. Might be one way to distinguish myself from the rest of the lumpen prols running around with cameras in this town, no?

At least I am *thinking* about such things, if not in fact acting upon them. Increments, an artist's originality is forged in increments. How's that for another empty aphorism to live by? God, I hate that word "artist." Fucking pretentious for someone so green to even presume to be worthy of such an aspiration. Although I'm sure I'd get an argument out of all those poor souls currently enrolled at the SVAs and RISDs of the world, not to mention all those art-school grads who now think they're waiters.

Decided to go up to the Museum of Natural History only to find it closed, leaving me stranded on the Upper Westside with nothing to do and no energy to do it. It was a gorgeous afternoon for wandering around the park, which is where I went—up a still rather verdant CPW—when I noticed two planes directly above me, flying somewhat irregularly.

It was soon apparent they were skywriting, or at least trying to. The day was clear and sun drenched, but a steady wind was breaking their ethereal letters apart not long after they took shape. A stranger soon approached, wondering if I had cracked the code. We both shrugged, as if to reassure each other it was no reflection certainly on our intelligence, but rather the adverse weather conditions we were up against.

Scratched heads cocked to the skies, we returned to our viewing stations. What were they trying to tell us? The more the planes toiled, the more baffling it became. Was it just another misguided Madison Avenue bid for our attention? If so, they had it, but what were they flogging, what was it we were supposed to be buying? The best my fellow cryptologist could come up with was it was a whimsical salutation extended to someone named "Johnson."

Personally, I wanted to believe it was the hand of some brimstone-breathing televangelist, a missive to fallen New Yorkers (which is to say *all* New Yorkers) from the god-fearing rest of the country, demanding we repent for all the evil we have brought upon the world. For the same-sex encounters on the piers, the narcotics, the twisted nightlife with its human toilets—repent for the perversity that festers and thrives in the Empire City like no place other.

Assuming then the sky *was* falling, that the end was indeed nigh, my only question for the man above was, Did I have enough time to beat it downtown to grab my dog and cameras? The answer was not forthcoming. Soundly defeated, we were about to part company when the high winds finally abated and

"Love, Yoko" could now clearly be seen suspended across the sky. The sphinx had spoken.

My colleague's "Johnson," we surmised, must have been a windswept "John" bleeding into "Sean." Standing less than a block from Family Lennon's Dakota digs, it certainly *seemed* plausible. And they were, were they not, about to release a long-awaited record? How better to jumpstart a dormant career than by taking to the skies above Media Central!

Skywriting over Manhattan seemed very much in character for a couple who never seemed particularly shy when it came to using the broad strokes of spectacle for shameless self-promotion. (Whither Bed-Ins . . . Hair Peace . . . ?) Yoko reiterating her already very public love for her man might not only help reinstate Beatle John in the minds of the record-buying public but also bring new life to that cult of personality fetishism the two always seemed so ready to court.

And how was all this playing up Dakota way? Was John done up in his apron, kneading his macrobiotic dough when wifey's celestial love comes floating across the kitchen window? Or maybe he was busy catching up on his Soaps and Yoko bursts in, turns off that infernal box and insists he join her for a walk in the park.

"John . . . in the sky . . . what dat?"

"Not sure, Muther . . . Johnson . . . ?"

The scenarios were endless, the mystery ever deepening. What remained of the afternoon could only be anti-climactic.

## He's Only Sleeping
October 10, 1980
9:25 A.M.

Am sick of waking up to TV test patterns in the middle of the night, still in my clothes, splayed across the couch like a certain unemployed (unemployable?) actor I'm still trying to forget. What happened to maintaining the integrity of the day, carpe diem, and all those other noble acts of self-discipline I keep promising my various selves I'm going to start adhering to? Shouldn't complain—at least I'm getting *some* sleep, regardless of how unceremonious it may be.

Saw Yoko's "sky piece" on the news last night just before falling off. Not only do John and Sean share the same birthday, but yesterday was Papa Bear's 4-0. Yoko apparently had the two planes continuously write "Happy Birthday" until they ran out of whatever it is they use to write with up there. All was for naught, however, as John reportedly spent the afternoon in bed, deep in the arms of Morpheus.

Best to let sleeping Beatles lie, me thinks, particularly on their birthday. At least *someone* is getting their proper rest.

### The Committee of Sleep

October 12, 1980

7:45 A.M.

Chronic fatigue has begun to set in—haven't had a good night's in days. Overheard someone talking while cooling my heels outside The Saint about some Taiwanese artist who is in the middle of a year-long performance where every hour on the hour he stops whatever he's doing (including sleeping) and punches a time clock. And I thought I was unsettled.

Marvin tells me not to worry, insomnia is the disorder of the serious, I should see it as a tribute to my determination. All those who have ever busied themselves thinking the big thoughts have been insomniacs at one time or another according to him—Dickens, Kafka, Edison, even Nixon. Although, in Nixon's case, it was probably a heightened sense of injustice linked with a heavy dose of persecution complex that kept him awake.

That's all well and good, Mr. Marvin, compliment accepted even if we both know you're a slyboots with an agenda, but can we be honest here, if only for a moment? No one, myself included, has ever thought of me as a particularly serious person—the world is serious enough, without me adding to the mix, doncha know.

What I *am* serious about though is my sleep. For the last week or so, since Monsieur Bob in point of fact, it has become an ongoing battle to get five—even four—hours. Moreover, what sleep I do manage is stooge sleep. Not that of the deep, refreshing variety but the sort that's just enough to turn you into a bumbler, the kind that instantly sinks an already circumscribed attention span like mine.

Must be all that adrenaline surging through my system, triggered by the fascination/fear of the arrival of the new and novel. The mere *possibility* of romance is evidently enough to muck with my auto-immune system. Simply put, the very prospect of a "him" is keeping me up at night, replete with dreams (or rather nightmares) wherein he takes on a variety of guises some alarming, others plain fiendish à la the Trickster. Can't tell whether what's between us is real or if it's the sound of one hand clicking, just me and my "want," that deep abiding need to connect, projected onto yet another seemingly receptive man.

Was finally on the verge of falling back off to sleep late this morning when the buzzer rang. Tom the Postman had some magazines for me from the return-to-sender pile. Sweet. As mailmen go he couldn't be nicer, but, still, there is something more than a little creepy about a guy who claims to have had an irrational fear of clowns since childhood. And that's not the half of it.

Should we run into each other before I've made it to my box, he will, without fail, characterize my day's spoils, then list each piece of mail in descending order of importance. Either the man has a photographic memory or, for reasons known only to him, he's taken a special interest in *my* mail.

Perhaps it's some twisted kind of mailman flirtation device, trying to relate through what they've brought you. But that's just the point. If your mailman's paying attention, as obviously this one is, he can create a deceptively accurate profile just on what he's placed in your box. You are, in essence, the sum total of your correspondences. Compounding that sense of invasion is the fact he knows exactly where you live!

Can't believe I just wrote that! A good night's rest and such paranoid piffle would never have lodged itself in my brain and onto the page. Such is the fate of the sleep-deprived, always looking to foist meaning where none belongs. Besides, this guy has a wife to whom he's hopelessly devoted for a multitude of reasons, not least of which must be that she apparently likes to go to sleep with "it" in her mouth. Have to believe such unyielding oral dedication to the male member is a rare and beautiful thing, this coming from someone for whom the American Handshake has always been more about paying lip service than actual tribute. But is this the kind of small talk you should be having with your mailman?

You can't choose your mailman, just as you can't choose your parents, but I wish to god this guy would single out someone else to impress. Not that I'm not flattered in some strange, unseemly sort of way, mind you.

Sometimes to survive in the jungle you have to play dead—maybe if I avoid him long enough he'll start obsessing over someone else's box. Perhaps I should stay in bed for a few days and not get out for anyone or thing, including my mail.

**Trumped**

Either the night life ain't what it used to be in this town or it was a very slow evening at the assignment desk—the *Post* actually had me covering a dinner dance last night celebrating the renovation of the old Commodore Hotel next to Grand Central. They've refitted the place with a shiny new skin of reflective glass and rechristened it "The Grand Hyatt," confirming just how subjective that word can be ("grand" not "Hyatt").

If you're suffering from a terminal case of disco fever or jonesing for the return of the singles fern bar à la Maxwell's Plum, then "grand" it is. Others, I should think, are bound to see it differently. To these eyes, the place looks like an overstuffed Halston showroom better suited to the likes of Liza with a "z" or Bianca Nicaragua than Mr. and Mrs. Out-of-Towner.

It was murky to me why the *Post* would be interested in the opening of such a Spirit of '76 tangle of chrome and mirrors. Rather than the usual room full of boldfaces to work with, I was stuck with mostly contractors and politico-fixer types. At the center of it all stood our own good Governor Carey, who was nervously pressing as much flesh as time would allow, no doubt lining up a gentle landing in his soon-to-be new home, the private sector.

The evening came to what would ultimately have to be considered its "climax" when the host—the developer behind the abomination—finally made his entrance. Sporting a bad haircut and roguish sneer, it didn't take long for the scuttle-butt to start flying. The guy was an egomaniac, an insurrectionist, the heathen who jackhammered the Bonwit Teller sculptures into dust, etc., etc. The tall drink of glitzy blonde on his arm only served as more cannon fodder for the self-appointed guardians of the city's architectural gates. To hear it from some, The Vandals not only had crashed the barriers, they had out and out commandeered the palace.

Evidently, this is not the last we will hear from this guy. Word is he's bought Tiffany's air rights with the intention of putting up a luxury shopping center cum high-rise condo next door. The kicker is he's naming it after himself. As Mom's cousin, the very fetching Dorthea, used to say about every suitor who came calling after her husband died, "The man ain't nuthin' but a gorilla in a party dress!"

## He Called
October 16, 1980
9:03 A.M.

The question as to whether I gave Monsieur Bob my number has now been answered—I didn't. He found a way to get it anyway, which is not *necessarily* a bad thing—we must admire the enterprising—but what exactly he's after (much like what he has or hasn't had) is still unclear.

Our story begins with my dropping the contacts off at Bunty's. Everyone seemed thrilled, Marcy so much so she apparently showed them to the Boy (still don't understand what's going on between those two or am I just being wantonly naïve?), who was thrilled enough to tell Bunty he wants to hire me—would she give him my number? Bunty had the courtesy to clear it with me first, but what was I going to say, no?

So Monsieur calls yesterday not with an assignment but with the suggestion we go clubbing—turns out he's a D.J. (Did he tell me that last time?) who can get us on "the list," any list. Was there someone I'd like to see?

"Roy Orbison at the Lone Star."

"Roy who?"

"You know . . . Blue Bayou . . ."

"You mean Linda Rondstadt . . ?"

For a D.J. his American pop history is not exactly deep, but after a brief lecture on the wonder that is Roy, he decided he would take my word for it.

So, it's a date. An actual, sit/wait/pull-out-your-hair date. Can't remember the last time I was out on one of those, if ever. I'm trying to think of this as a variation on the "rebound": find a younger, entirely unsuitable guy (preferably foreign) with whom to work through your sexual frustrations before throwing yourself back into the pond in earnest. The provincial equivalent of when Mary ran away to Nassau the week after Leon left, what she called "The Club Med Solution."

Have two days now to get myself worked up over all of this. When do I start worrying about what to wear? Do I keep him guessing and do something subtle, like henna my hair? With my luck it would only make me look older. So many questions, so much time to drive one crazy.

### The Club Med Solution

October 18, 1980

7:54 A.M.

Just got in from the big date and I must say, once I got over the terror of *being* on a date, I think I actually started to enjoy myself. And what's the first thing I take out when I get home? Why dear diary, of course! Must be a schoolgirl trapped somewhere deep inside that feels this compelled to commit every little detail to paper. It's almost eight in the morning and everyone I want to spout off to is either fast asleep or getting ready for work. Alone again, naturally.

Where to begin? Fucked him. Am sure of it this time. It was good. When the guy is energetic, always hard, and doesn't want to stop until his partner is dog-tired satisfied, how can it be anything but? Been a while since I've had that bow-legged, just-been-run-over-by-a-truck-and-loved-it feeling. At thirty-five, B never seemed old to me, until last night. Which, of course, leaves both Lech and Marvin crusty and far, far beyond the pale although with the hordes of hormones that are now coursing so madly through my system, anything and everyone seems possible. Could get addictive, this Club Med Solution.

Orbison was exalted, Dorian Gray in shades. Looked like he had stepped right off an early '60s album cover. Same haircut, same dark glasses but, most importantly, same haunted, other-worldly voice. Doesn't seem to have lost *anything* range-wise. With all those high Cs he hits it's more bel canto than rock 'n' roll, which gives the music that genre blur and makes it hard to pigeonhole. Hacks for a backing band but it would be more than churlish to complain.

We were huddled right up front, so I knew I'd be able to shoot at least a roll before anyone figured out what I was up to, let alone be able to get to me. The Boy's aptly dubbed "Rainbow Choke" had me so high I thought I was hallucinating. By the time Roy dedicated "Pretty Woman" to "the lady down front with the camera," I *knew* I was hallucinating. Between the pot and my own well-developed narcissism, it felt like every eye in the house was on me. No longer able to hold the camera steady, I ceased and desisted of my own accord.

On the way out, as if to fan the flames of paranoia, some guy comes up from behind and starts haranguing about how he once saw Little Richard walk off stage because someone was taking his picture without his permission and he refused to come back until the guy was thrown out. You forget sometimes how threatening the camera can be, particularly to those who like to control their image, even if it's that very image that helps endear the paying public to them in the first place.

Not sure Roy made much of an impression on Monsieur Bob. He seemed far more fascinated with the Lone Star and the idea of transposing a Texas bar onto lower Fifth, of the myth of the American West appropriated and reconfigured into a theme park for New Yorkers. You don't need to be a foreigner to have that odd sense of displacement in a room full of urban cowboys whooping it up over long neck beers. Personally, I blame J. Travolta: first disco fever, now this . . . what has thou wrought, Barbarino??!!

Hopped a cab down to West Broadway and TR3, a snug, sliver of a place. Suffice it to say, I now know how it feels to dance drunk in a submarine. Didn't catch who the bands were, it was between sets, but the D.J. must have been a Brit because he had that Jamaican Dub thang down. (Monsieur's assessment, not mine, although I couldn't agree more, not because I know what he's talking about, but because I'm feeling so agreeable at the moment.)

We looked in on a very not happening Mudd, and quickly split, leaving it to Jersey and Westchester to sift through what remains of that moldering acropolis of cool. From there it was up to 23rd Street and Squat where the Boy's favorite band (whose name I've already forgotten) was supposedly about to go on at two or until they sold the bar dry, whichever came last.

Monsieur immediately disappeared upstairs to "look for friends," leaving me in the middle of an attitude exhibition. No simple anarchist black for these lot, this was a carefully orchestrated, do-it-yourself time twist done mostly in quotes: baggy suits and fedoras for the men, tight tube dresses and baubles for the ladies. Affected more as homage than straight retro referencing, most in the room had clearly been boning up on their film noir with a select few looking to the Weimar Republic for that harder, Euro-centric edge.

Feeling underdressed and abandoned, I finally worked up enough nerve to track the ever-elusive Corsican up the stairs. At the top was a red satin curtain that I blithely walked through only to realize I'd entered someone's apartment. There was an actress (Hungarian?) I thought I recognized sprawled across a couch. Uninvited guest that I was, I quickly turned around to go back down when she asks if I'm looking for "Robert." Does *everyone* know this guy?

She points me to a backroom where a large group is crowded around a glass counter, a rogues' table strewn with white rails of powder. Again, my natural reaction is to turn around but too late—"Robert" calls me over, introductions are made. The "backstage" party had been on for a while judging from the incessant chitter-chatter. The Flying Lizards record on the stereo was barely audible above all the quasi-profundities. When the woman from the couch entered to tell the band their public was getting restless, they reached for their fedoras, checked their bad selves (and noses) in the mirror, and it was showtime.

I can see why he likes them, the music's a kind of urban noize swing. Their point of reference may be jazz, but they owe as much to Stockhausen as Monk. Monsieur Bob was clearly in his element, as least until the coke wore off. Me, I was more than a bit preoccupied wondering what bit of non-sense the aftershow might hold. It didn't matter so much *where* we went just as long as we went, far, far away from the scenesters and their vials.

First stop? Some LES, after-hours dive. Not my choice. Obviously. When the cops suddenly appear, the proprietress leads us in an impromptu chorus of "Happy Birthday," then promptly sweet-talks the Boys in Blue into believing it's not a speakeasy they've stumbled on, but rather a late-night party among friends.

Agreeing we've just lived our ninth life, Monsieur Bob suddenly gets smart and suggests we watch the sunrise from The Clocktower, a real, believe-it-or-not tower with a clock on lower Broadway that they're in the middle of converting to an alternative space.

We cab it down to Leonard and saunter into the building as if on our way to work. The droopy marshmallow at the front desk yells after us to sign his log, to which the Boy responds by entering us as N & J Bonaparte—Corsican pride dies hard. Just that easy, just that quick, we're in; a couple of imperialist worker bees getting a jump on the rest of the workaday world.

An elevator and spiral staircase later and we're in the middle of the tower, up to our eyes in the internal machinations of this huge four-sided clock, a jumble of gears and ballasts moving at an almost imperceptible pace. From there, it was exit stage left through a lead door and out onto the roof deck.

Waiting for the sun and the spirit of Jim Morrison, but more importantly it's waiting for the Boy to make his move. Assuming he *has* a move. Monsieur is waning, on the verge of nodding out. And if something doesn't happen soon we'll *both* be asleep.

"We can just go home, you know," I whisper, almost relieved to hear myself offering him (and me) the out.

"No, no . . . let's stay—I want to stay," he mumbles, struggling to hold his head up and meet my eyes. Alain Delon he's not right now, more like a stupefied Pepé Le Pew.

I'm not even sure why I am here any more, but at this hour the why of it no longer seems important. I decide to make my lack of sleep my alcohol, my morning-after excuse and let his hard-body youth justify anything else that may need justification. I mean, how could it, the two of us getting together, be about anything *other* than lust?

I would love nothing more than to trust this man/boy, open up to him, but more out of force of habit than hope for the future. It's a strange feeling, the compulsion to fight the emotional investment—is this what it's like for men?

My patience expended and in the interest of time, I silently move to straddle him, fumbling for his belt. He doesn't seem to mind and as his level of arousal increases so does his assertiveness.

Gently, he places me up on the railing. It's all I can do to keep from falling, which, of course, means I have to drive myself onto him that much harder. If ever there was a time when I thought I was going to have an O without the practical prompting from a finger or two this was it. Was so taken out, in fact, I forgot to turn around when the sun finally did come up. A small price to pay for one's pleasure.

Later, it's back to his place for more morning madness, which is where I must have run into that truck. Or was it a motorcycle?

### Frank World
October 23, 1980
10:23 A.M.

To me, the either/or concept of hero/villain was always quaint, almost Victorian in its absolutism. Chasing bold-faces for the past month had made me even more convinced of that notion. And then I saw Frank.

Much to the consternation of more than one friend who thinks I should know better, I never really "got" Frank. Frank belonged to your parents, he was the guy they slow danced to, before they had you. By the time I was growing up he was an aging hipster with an overreaching ego who did bad Beatle covers, wore laughable hairpieces, and went into phony retirements. In Rat-Pack speak, Ol' Blue Eyes was not my "bag."

Sinatra's new movie premiered last night, his first in something like ten years. Like most of his movies, it's probably not very good—were they ever?—but that's not the point.

This guy's not just a major artist/personality, he's a major dude, which I guess is what makes him such an easy target and why he has come to loathe bottom-feeder cameras-for-hire like myself with such venom.

Last night, staking him out with the faithful in front of the Ziegfield (or should I add the "l" and make it "stalking?") I began to get a better understanding of the public's fascination. The cross section of people alone was telling: jazzbos mingling with aging, defeated bobbysoxers, autograph hounds, and the just plain curious, all looking to see if the man could possibly make good on the myth.

When he finally did arrive, even his co-star Faye Dunaway seemed overwhelmed by the throng's reaction. In his sixties by now, Frank's no longer the "presence" he must have been in his day, but it wasn't his presence alone that had the faithful so riled. I've seen enough famous faces to know the effect they can have on a crowd, and this was decidedly something else.

Simply put, his kind of celebrity is sui generis, he is a public figure unto himself. There's no publicity machine, no image maker out there powerful enough to *create* a Frank Sinatra. Everything he has, he's created himself, *including* his persona. And because he is his own creation he can be his own man in a way all the others can't, which is probably why the believers are so impassioned—why those who love him do so with such boundless fervor. They know this guy, he's like them and their friends, with all the blemishes and contradictions still intact and in plain view.

It's those very same character flaws and arrogances that alienate others, the ones who expect their stars to serve as some kind of role model, to be better than they are. When you hobnob with mob bosses, pimp for Presidents, abandon your family for a starlet, etc., you're bound to draw *someone's* ire. J. Edgar Hoover kept a running file on Frank until the day Hoover died for Chrissakes!

Ultimately, it's Sinatra's ability to stay ahead of his appetites that I admire. I think I may have it backwards, for unlike the vast majority, it's not the music or movies but the man—the no-bullshit, fuck-with-me-and-I'll-fuck-with-you, Hoboken-goomba attitude that attracts me. It's enough to make your slow-dancing parents proud, albeit for all the wrong reasons.

I know what *I* think of Frank, so what does Frank think of me? He's never made a secret of his contempt for the press, especially paparazzi, has even clocked one or two in his day. As the newly minted, (hardly) working camera-for-hire that I am, can we then complete the syllogism and declare it safe to assume Frank hates me? And just as I'm finally coming to admire him.

The Sinatra experience has got me wondering how the hell it is I've so quickly joined the ranks of the hated and reviled. It's the cabbage, of course—wasn't as if it was forced on me. Can we just wonder out loud why we love something less once we start getting paid for it, and leave it at that?

## What Is in a Name

October 28, 1980

9:32 A.M.

Have not done much as of late to further my cause, my so-called struggle out of oblivion. The more this indolence-induced guilt mounts, the more paralyzing it becomes. Haven't really shot anything for myself since the Lolitas and even that was with one eye on trying to sell it to some fucking rag. What pains is it's not even journalism I'm aspiring to but the gossip pages, celeb hunting, pure twaddle. My, but how far the mighty can fall given half a chance.

Reminds me of that Dylan put-down—once the folk scare had safely subsided—when he declared Phil Ochs to be nothing more than a journalist before forcing him out of the limo and off the gravy train. Call me "Miss Ochs" if you like, Lord knows I've earned it, and Miss Ochs regrets she's unable to work today due to a severe case of listlessness. Beware, beware, the sloth doth return.

Since no one seems to give a monkey's if I pick up my camera or not, I guess I'd prefer not to. Fine, Bartleby, as you wish.

Am wearing my new Picasso t-shirt today, the one with his signature I bought in front of the MOMA. What strikes me most about the thing (aside how fab I look in it with my exposed navel) is the perfection of the name "Pablo Picasso." It fits the man's face to a "t," the alliteration serves as a mnemonic plus, *plus*, it gives great pleasure coming off the tongue. "Pablo Picasso"—an oral/aural orgasm for the mouth and ears.

Which of course begs the question: What kind of name is M. L. Weeks? Where's the tingle in that? What if I were to lose the initials and insist everyone call me "Mary Louise" from now on? Sounds like a happy homemaker who should be busy cooking and cleaning for her ungrateful brood. I can't cook, can barely keep myself fed with take-out, and as for my brood . . . I rest my case, your Honor.

All of this is by way of leading into the SF punk rag I saw the other day with a pic of Jello Biafra surfing the dance pit at The Mabuhay. The credit read "F-stop Fitzgerald." The picture was serviceable at best, but fuck! What a brilliant *nom de guerre*, not just for its literary pretensions but for the pun which ensures you won't forget who took the shot, even if you don't like the picture. I'm beginning to see that sometimes having a brilliant name, much like having a brilliant title for your movie is half the battle when it comes to making yourself known above the din. Witness "Jello Biafra."

Maybe *that's* what's not working or, put another way, why I am not working (enough)—I need a new name, something that cues you in that this is the chick for the job. And maybe then can come a clean break from this desultory, post-collegiate present that doesn't seem to want to transform itself into something else, something more . . . professional. Growing weary waiting for that second-stage rocket to appear and thrust me into a different, more elevated orbit. Higher ground.

Of course F-stop and Jello aren't the first to play the name game. Emerson, Thoreau, Dylan—they all wrapped their personas in a fiction of their own devise, not forgetting my favorite, St. Paul. Do you think they'd have made him a saint had he not dropped the Saul? St. Saul . . . ???? Not that I'm bucking for sainthood here, Lord knows, but why should Mary Louise Weeks have to be saddled with Mary Louise Weeks the rest of her life?

Let us not forget the woman who was born "Eve" but changed her name to "Fred" as an act of solidarity with all the Freds of the world who were suffering from low self-esteem because they had had to answer to "Fred" their entire lives. May I propose at this juncture she could have just as easily changed her name to "Mary Louise" along similar lines of reasoning without having to cross the gender line.

Why wait any longer? Even Freud got the importance of one's name on the psyche, if not soul. How does "Joan Parallax" scan? Or maybe Jane Vanishing Point? Fanny Fixer? Ready for my transformation, Mr. DeMille!


## Another Bullet Dodged

November 1, 1980

1:34 P.M.

Lech called late yesterday afternoon to tell me that the much ballyhooed Plato's reopening had once again been postponed, something about problems with permits. Permits for what, multiple partners? Secretly relieved, I saw no need to let on that the prospect of a fright night fraught with (im)perfectly naked strangers was beginning to set me off my feed as the bewitching hour fast approached.

In lieu of "swinging," he suggested we take the Mustang and haunt the streets for parties to crash. As I think I've stated in these pages before, I love Lech dearly and I'd like to believe it's mutual, but riding aimlessly around with him Halloween night seemed just short of a death wish. So I begged off, telling him I was going to stay home with my dog and a good book. Incredibly enough, he bought it, and we left it at that.

Staying in was never an option, the only real question was whether I could muster enough enthusiasm to make it over to Bank Street for yet another year to shoot the Village parade. How many drag queens can one portfolio possibly sustain before collapsing from all that good-natured camp? As the parade's raison d'être, queens have become for me what ghettos were for Spiro Agnew: see one and you've pretty much seen them all. This year's crop of hirsute lovelies was going to have to make due with one less prodding camera because *this* year I was finally going to throw together a costume and actually *participate*.

After deciding on something that had me looking like a cross between a droog and a demonic Pinocchio, I was almost out the door when, quite impulsively, I picked up the phone and tried Monsieur Bob. Wonders would not cease (!) when he—not his machine—answered and, without hesitation, agreed to join me. A date for Halloween! And so easy! Should have realized then and there something was terribly amiss.

(Question: Is it still considered a date if you've already slept together or is "dating" simply code for casual, noncommittal sex? Clarification please, Miss Manners.)

The evening started to tailspin early, at his building's door actually, where the key-thrown-down-in-the-sock trick is required to get in. Yelling up wasn't getting his attention, so it was off to another block where I thought I remembered seeing a pay phone. No speaker in the handset—couldn't hear a word he was or wasn't saying. When I finally locate a phone that will take my dime, true to form, the machine picks up. Running out of options, I take aim at his window with small pieces of crumbling curb, but, evidently, short of the sound of breaking glass, nothing is going to bring him to the window. Was about to give up when someone suddenly pops out of the building, and I'm able to furtively catch the door with my foot. Not wanting to negotiate the antiquated (freight) elevator, I scramble up the three flights to an open door where there under the Harley, suggestively supine across an unmade bed, lay the beloved.

"Bon soir, Monsieur . . ."

He's oblivious—not until I'm actually hovering over him is he even aware of my presence.

"Hey there . . . were you sleeping?"

No response. Undaunted (or just hopelessly smitten), I bend down to kiss him only to find an ashen face, beaded in sweat.

"Where's Walter?" he wants to know.

"He's not in his box?"

The Boy hasn't prepared a costume, remembers nothing of my having called and quickly loses interest in "conversation." He wants only to sleep but everything's sore, his head's throbbing, his bulging eyes burning. The flu, he offers weakly.

He keeps asking for Walter until I finally make it plain that unless his roommate is hiding in his coffin, he must be gone. This turns him indignant, insisting I play sentry at the window and watch for him, as if it's my fault the guy's not here.

The aches and pains, the brain fog, this "Waiting for My Man" scenario . . . I may be stupid, Monsieur Bob, but I'm not dumb—I grew up in Manhattan, remember? What's ailing you is not the flu but junk, or more precisely, the lack thereof. Junk flu.

Surely there is no quicker way to torpedo a budding romance than to accuse the new flame of using. Even if you happen to be right, he will in all likelihood deny it; that's part of using, its unwritten ethos. On the other hand, do I want to be involved with someone involved with dope? Do I really want to get in on that threesome?

Keep fixating on Sid and Nancy's sojourn at the Chelsea and how *that* ended, which only confuses me more. Decide it's easier not to decide and simply do as I am told. Walter, come back already! The longer you stay away, the harder it is to ignore my patient and his disquiet.

By the time the convulsions begin, I realize my neglect is no longer benign. The time has come, I fear, to get him his fix. When I acknowledge I know what's up, he's nonchalant, interrupting his demon wrestling long enough to declare himself too pained to walk. He'll gladly explain where to go, though. And as long as we're being so open with each other, could I front him some money?

A Halloween adventure down Heroin Alley—what more could a white girl possibly ask of her middle-class existence? Riding shotgun with Lech looking for parties to crash suddenly doesn't seem quite the wanton folly it did at first blush.

To know you is to love you, poor dear Monsieur, your every wish my command, but if half the thrill of doing drugs is in the scoring, why should I have all the fun? I'll go *with* you, and yes, I'll even pay for it, but I cannot go there alone, wherever in God's name "there" may be. The family that cops together stays together—make yourself presentable and I promise, we will get you something to help you feel better.

The very real prospect of finally getting some dope brings new life to the Boy, bringing him onto his feet and over to the mirror. As he tries in vain to piece himself back together, I come up from behind with his blue blazer, place it atop his shoulders like a French film star and voilà! we're off: one completely gone Delon with his Big Nurse in tow.

The fresh air and adrenaline quickly converge in his bloodstream to return at least a *veneer* of cogency. He's embarrassed by his display, promises it won't happen again, all the while insisting that he's not hooked but simply experimenting, a "weekend warrior." I want to point out that it's only Wednesday but see no purpose in calculated antagonism now and soldier on in silence.

Mr. Coffin, a.k.a. Walter the Disappeared, to whom this untidy job of copping was supposed to fall, has obviously gone missing with the money, but the Boy now seems genuinely less preoccupied with what's happened to his cash than with his friend's fate. Not that personal safety is a *problem* where we're headed, he's quick to reassure.

And yet that nasty little problem of money persists. Offering myself up as his banker came not from compassion but unadulterated self-interest. It was, after all, my premarital bliss at stake here, nothing if not ironic when considering how dope doesn't exactly send one into fits of erotic abandon. Hopefully I had enough to get him what he needed and then some, like mad money for the cab fare out of there, should things prove too "colorful."

By the time we make it to Avenue C, I realize we're not the only strangers to come calling today. BMWs from Connecticut, Jersey Firebirds, even a limo has joined the parade, endlessly circling around the mostly abandoned streets in search of today's ad hoc dispensary. The Caravan of the Doomed, looking for a fall.

Ten minutes in and the sense of being out of my depth is starting to take over. Monsieur Bob can't seem to pick up the scent, and the stronger his craving, the more pronounced his frustration, which is not lost on the few locals dotting the stoops. They're needling him in Spanish, calling him "Poppi," bantering among themselves, creating a general sense of unease. Or so it seems to me.

Fuck the Boy and his fix, get me back on terra firma, get me back on the other side of A, at the Kiev, tucking into a bowl of mushroom barley. The comfort of soup is what *I'm* craving.

Monsieur explains we should be on the alert for any number of possible setups, depending on the level of police pressure. Had today been a cop-free day, the entire neighborhood would by now be a giant bazaar where the very glint of pale skin would bring out the sellers reflexively. In a somewhat "thicker" atmosphere, one where patrol cars have been seen rolling in the general vicinity, underage runners immune from the law will take your money and return minutes later with the goods. But any suspicion of unmarked cars or plain-clothes in the vicinity and only the best-versed of users—not suburbanites on a flirt but those long-since married to the stuff—are going to ID that car trunk or slatted door as having somebody behind it willing to sell to you.

While my dilettante roots may be showing, Monsieur Bob is not making things any easier by snarling every time the

Stoop People launch an epithet our way. I know the tooth-lessness of his threats, but how to impart this to the Stoops before it's too late, assuming we haven't passed that point already?

As I quietly prepare to get my candied ass kicked, there instantly appears from the sky a bucket on a rope, descending from the roof of the shell of a building next to us. To the neophyte, a bucket on a rope, though somewhat odd, is still just that, a bucket on a rope. But to initiates it's apparently a veritable lifeline, a real-life deus ex machina.

The Boy beelines to the thing, grabbing it before it can touch ground. My two crumpled tens go in "as is," and with a tug or two he sends it back up. Seconds later, like some profane alchemy, the bucket reappears, heavy with the magic bullets. Elated, he comes running back to me, the proud papa of two small paper triangles stamped with a skull and bones insignia above the word "juicy."

The "juicy" part sounds innocuous enough, it's the skull and bones that has pricked my ears. *Every* street drug requires a certain act of faith certainly, but the active courting of death is pure junkie hubris, the Romantic badge of courage worn in grim celebration of the possibilities. Everybody wants that fate-tempting shit, the stuff that just OD'd the last guy because, unlike the last guy, *they* know how to sneak up to Eternity without actually crossing over *into* it. Forget religion, Karl, *opiates* are the opiates of the people. Or at least a certain kind of people.

Monsieur Bob may not be exempt from such delusions. He wants another fiver for works, which is disturbing as somehow I had, rather hopefully I'll admit, pegged my "weekend warrior" as a chipper/snorter type, not the kind to get caught up in the messiness of needles, veins, and blood.

The route to the works is shorter than expected, but somewhere between flights of stairs a human roadblock suddenly appears, demanding to know our destination. Monsieur Bob looks upward to the heavens, to which the Hulking Man gestures for us to show him our arms. I get busy playing dumb while Monsieur Bob rolls up his sleeves and points to some red marks by his elbow—the doleful confirmation I didn't want to have to see.

In times of inner-conflict we tend to create stories that allow us to get through, to get on with it. My particular story had Monsieur Bob as a dabbler temporarily under water, but a dabbler nevertheless. With his sleeves now up and arms extended, however, it's plain he, the man with whom I want to occupy my time, is, in no uncertain terms, a doper. And he's sticking himself back by his elbow precisely so not even an intimate will catch on.

Having established his membership in the club, it's "Blondie's" turn to prove she's real. (Note to self: dye hair dark before next visit—the H aesthetic seems to have little use for the fair.) Clueless, I find myself resorting to my standard male-baiting technique and start unzipping my jumpsuit as if I'm shooting in my chest, in the hope, I guess, that the twins will distract this guy long enough for me to come up with something more definitive.

The Boy senses my bewilderment, zips me back up and simply pulls me past the guy, muttering about my being a snorter, or something to that effect, it's hard to say, as by now brain-freeze has taken over.

Convinced we're on the right floor only because we've run out of them, Monsieur is having trouble remembering which door we're looking for until we see an older, sway-backed Hispanic man slowly shuffling out of an apartment at the end of the hall. A mamacita peers at us from behind him, silently waving us to her before redirecting the rubber-legged man away from the wall and back down the hall. I can't tell if it's the Boy, or our being lost in a place where we don't belong that she recognizes, either way, she knows we're one of hers, a fact I can't quite find comfort in.

Lit candles line the railroad apartment, even though late afternoon sunlight is still straining through the windows. A crucifix hangs above the bathtub that takes up most of the kitchen in the front room. Deeper into the inner sanctum, the Virgin Mary beckons from her perch atop a TV that silently bathes the proceedings in cathode blue.

The place has all the markings of a typical LES home—save for the ten or so "guests" in various states of narcosis, splayed across a series of stained mattresses along the wildly sloping floor. Mamacita sits alone on the overstuffed couch, directing her "assistant" (daughter?) with one eye to the TV and the other on us.

The girl retrieves two sets of works from a kitchen cabinet but Monsieur gestures to her with a single finger, which draws wary eyes—those that are still open—all around. I'm not a narc, I want to assure them, but there's only one way to actually *prove* that, and it ain't about to happen. Whatever curiosity I may have had to try a taste has all but dissipated with this adventure.

Monsieur fumbles through his pockets for the plasticine envelopes which he opens up into a blackened spoon while motioning me to light the Bunsen burner cooling on the kitchen table. I'm supposed to cook the stuff for him while he ties off and looks for a vein. Just keeping the bent spoon steady over the flame is difficult, made no easier by the unforgiving glower of the Virgin.

For his part, the Boy can't get a vein to pop and reluctantly hands the rubber hose to the daughter before she demands another fiver which I am to give to Mamacitia who is by now off her couch and hovering. So much for a cab ride out of here.

The needle piercing the skin, the blood drawing into the hypo, the look on his face as she boots the stuff into his bloodstream: I now know why they call it a "shooting gallery." If coke makes you want to get inside everybody's head, H must make you want to crawl back into yourself and ossify. It must create some kind of tunnel out from your immediate surroundings, which is why I guess it's the drug of choice in neighborhoods where crime is high and money short. And as violent as people may become to *get* the stuff, when they are in the middle of its throes there's an over-riding sense of peace. These guys laid out on their mattresses could be mummies, inert and perfectly preserved in a wash of unruffled self-possession. Sweet oblivion—no one can touch them here. Which is probably why, ironically enough, they'll go to such extremes to get the stuff.

When Mamacita decides their time is up, no one can get them up off the floor either—their muscles are too relaxed to want to function properly. Most lifers tend to look well-preserved for the same reason, the aging process just can't compete with all that relaxation of the facial muscles.

The prospect of the Boy going into a happy stupor on one of those dingy mattresses while I am left to watch the muted TV on the overstuffed couch with Mamacita becomes too much to bear, and I make my preemptive strike before we all get too comfortable. Not wanting to ruin his much belabored high, I gently shepherd him from his seat at the table to the door. He seems to sense my unease with my surroundings and doesn't fight me, in fact is rather pliable if not altogether steady on his feet.

We bid a fond farewell to our new acquaintances, and I lead him to the stairs, trying to get him into the rhythm of putting his left after his right after his left and so on down the six flights and back to the streets. It's too late to make it over to the West Village for the parade and cab fare back to his place is blown so there's nothing left to do but walk. If I could get him to my place without *too* much trouble he could relax, sleep, whatever it is you do after something like this, and then send him on his merry way come morning.

He's leaning on me, so much so that I start getting paranoid the cops are going to catch on and stop us for questioning until I eventually come to see that Monsieur's loping, stumbling gate is not unique in these parts. Not only has H become the driving force of the Alphabet economy but it's also a favorite pursuit of both residents and "visitors" alike. Koch's minions have quietly conceded everything east of A to whoever wants it, giving the place a frontier town atmosphere. High adventure, but an acquired taste to be sure.

We've made it as far as Thieves' Alley on Second Avenue a block above Kiev when the bottom falls out. There on the sidewalk, arranged in a most orderly fashion, is what must be the entire contents of Monsieur's closet. The peddler of these wares, standing proudly against a nearby wall, is none other than Walter, the roommate who not only disappeared with the money but who now has decided to hawk Monsieur's wardrobe and a dress or two (Bunty's daughter's?) for good measure. I try and point out what we've stumbled across, but the Boy is having enough trouble just remaining upright.

My heart is sinking. Whatever I may have felt for him/secretly hoped for us, it all leaves me at that very moment. To look at him is to see a total stranger, removing me not only from these sordid surroundings but from myself as well. How did

I run so far afield, what was I telling myself to justify taking up with someone so clearly out of control? (Or maybe not so clearly, at least in the beginning . . . right?) I love projects, it's the injured bird syndrome that the Florence Nightingale in me can't seem to resist, but this is one undertaking I simply can't afford to take on. Not now, not this time.

Still, I can't just leave the guy here on the street in a daze, stumbling over his own purloined clothes. Walter doesn't stick around long enough to even *try* and make an excuse, he sees us coming and he's gone, leaving me to gather the goods back into the Vuitton suitcase they came in.

By the time I've schlepped clothes and boy to my place I am so tired and disgusted I feel like leaving him on the street, but the maternal instinct takes hold and I tuck him into my bed instead. After I make him drink as much orange juice as he can possibly stand, he nods out almost immediately, beatific smile neatly painted across his face.

Some hours later, he wakes up apologizing; somehow aware our time together is limping to a close. I want to know why he didn't tell me earlier about the heroin. He hasn't an answer, other than to launch into a twisted tale of how he got started on it, as the kept boy of a famous fashion designer who provided him with a home and drugs in exchange for allowing the designer to masturbate while Monsieur sat around the house, naked. He makes a point of stressing the fact they never actually touched, as if that would somehow weaken my resolve. Interesting tale but not exactly the way to get the girl back.

If it has to end abruptly, best to end it now, before the attachment becomes too strong to simply crash and burn the thing and we get into one of those long, airless unravelings. (And before the historicism takes over, let's try and remember how ambiguous I was about this guy.)

As sad as I may *think* I am at the moment, let's also point out that, hopefully, I am now smart enough to recognize that after all those other failed attempts at making permanent what is by its very nature ephemeral, to have failed once again is not the end of the world, but in fact just the world turning. And, more than likely, another bullet dodged. Amen.

### Landslides
November 4, 1980
5:54 P.M.

It rained all day, not just because that's what the weatherman called for, but because that's the only thing it *could* do on a day like today, on a day this dark. Actually, it wasn't so much rain as a slow, inexorable pissing that drizzled down through dimmed skies and lacquered the streets with soggy resignation.

Everywhere I went the atmosphere seemed dulled with pregnant pause. All knew the facts, yet no one was quite ready to accept them. Perhaps if we refused to acknowledge what was happening, the reality would simply dissipate from sheer indifference.

The plan was to go to Marvin's and watch the returns come in from there. By mid-afternoon, I knew I'd be cowering under the covers instead. Carter certainly did all he could to assure his own demise, but I never thought he'd have his head handed to him quite like this. (Honesty and politics must make for strange bedfellows, or is that just being naïve?) Someone at The Kitchen must have seen it coming though. They chose tonight to screen tapes of the '76 returns rather than subject their guests to the present tense of today's debacle.

Showing tapes from the last election—the perfect solution. Drizzle dazzle drazzle drone, time for this one to come home! Mister Wizard, Mister Wizard, stow us away in your time machine and get us out of here, out from under this Orange County landslide.

9:43 P.M.

All the returns aren't in but they don't have to be—the result is more than official. Today the country settled for less and turned degenerate. Today we accepted, nay *embraced*, mediocrity in the guise of Reagan and his keepers. Dart, Annenberg et al. have now been handed the mandate they've been champing at the bit for ever since Ford squandered his political inheritance. These fuckers are going to soon resuscitate the kind of country the last twenty years was spent trying to bury. This isn't just a landslide, it's a backslide! Repeat after me class: "I . . . like . . . Ike."

Perhaps I'm overreacting, perhaps this is just our comeuppance. Praise the Lord and pass the ammunition, the Moral

Majority is alive and well and living in an America that has finally gotten what it deserves—a bad actor with great hair. Paris never looked so good!

## Heaven's Gate Can Wait
November 18, 1980
11:45 P.M.

Was supposed to cover the opening of the new Michael "Deer Hunter" Cimino movie tonight but United Artists got cold feet at the last minute and cancelled. The official word is the director needs more time with his editor, while rumor has it *no* amount of editing is going to save this donkey, already reported to be the most expensive movie made. Ever.

Someone at the *Post* said there was a "test screening" last week that didn't go so well. Can't say that I'm surprised; give a director an Oscar, then carte blanche on his follow-up, and what do you get? A Western on roller skates, or so word has it.

Not that I much care, about the movies that is. Almost every-thing coming out now seems to have an eye on not only trying to please *everyone,* but please them more than once. Repeat business is the new mantra. The problem is when they start expecting everyone to dream the same dream. Since when can you put a "consensus" on desire?

Studios keep feeding us tall tales of killer sharks and cuddly space creatures as if smaller-scaled stories about real people will no longer hold our attention. And when actual flesh and blood *is* given center stage, they're not so much actors adapting to the demands of the role, as personas being foisted down our throats. Whether they're right for the character or not is asked only as an afterthought, and only if the thing has tanked, once the finger pointing has begun.

J. Nicholson is the perfect example—he's no longer playing roles, he's playing "Jack." And the more pictures he makes, the more the "Jack" persona is reinforced until finally all pretense of a "character" disappears completely. W. Benjamin's "spell of personality" in a nutshell, I guess. (Always knew that Ivy League education would some day prove good for *something*, like being able to recognize when what you're taking to be your own argument is in fact a parroting of someone else's.)

All of which has me wondering about my own complicity in the star-making machinery. When it came to reinforcing the cult of personality required for an "active" celebrity culture, the old Hollywood was very good at controlling what did and didn't get out for public consumption. Now that everyone is an enterprise unto themselves, *everything* is fair game. And all the scandal and rumor mongering that comes with it only plays to photography's strengths—its "objectivity." To wit: If you see a picture of Farrah kissing Ryan then they *must* be a couple. Right?

On the other hand, in a world of shimmering surfaces photography is the master illusionist where image is all—whatever may lie beneath the superficial is irrelevant. So the picture has it covered from both sides, and editors work that ambiguity to serve their own purposes, without restraint. Let's face it—would *People* have been the biggest selling magazine this year if it *didn't* run photos?

Having said that, I have to acknowledge I, too, play it from both sides. My camera can get me into places I wouldn't otherwise have access to, be it a premiere or a prison. It's just another form of wish fulfillment really, something akin to an actor taking on a role—you delve into another life for a finite length of time without having to actually commit to it. It brings out the schizophrenic in you, while at the same time hopefully broadens your understanding of the world.

But at what price? At what point does it become exploitive? That's what galls so about the whole celebrity thing. "Personality" photogs are little more than parasites, cashing in on the celebrity of others and the public's thirst to be close to them.

When the assignment is this week's flavor, mine is a rote response: get the shot and get out. I've now done enough shoots of dubious import to know when the real deal slips through. That's when you become that much more aware just how invasive the job really is, how much of a parasite you really are—especially if they don't need you like you need them. Like Sinatra.

A girl's gotta do what a girl's gotta do to get by in this world, granted, but deep down there's a dark feeling churning around somewhere that I need to get out of this paparazzi shtick before I completely take my eye off the prize. And let us not forget that the less time I have to dream and make those unlikely connections between things, the harder it will be to get back into the flow of the creative act.

Duly noted and good night!

### Who'll Buy My Memories
November 20, 1980
5:52 P.M.

Run in on Canal this afternoon. Don't know where I found the pluck to be so confrontational on a street known for its surfeit of the unhinged, but there I was, calling out some "picker" (as Martyr would call him) for being the lowlife he was.

It began innocently enough—I woke up too late to get the special at that greasy spoon on Spring/Crosby (just down from Bing/Crosby) so decided to cheer myself up with a new—that is to say old—leather jacket. When Sailor Jack turned pirate over something I wasn't that interested in anyway, I took the hint and continued across Canal and the Saturday flea, looking for that guy with the racks of stuff from the '50s.

He wasn't in his usual spot, which either meant he woke up later than me, or he wasn't coming. Given how cold it was I couldn't blame him if he simply rolled over and went back to sleep. Decided to give him more time and was meandering around some tables where a series of boxes filled with "amateur" photos catches my attention. I browse through a few not too terribly interesting collections of random portraits and travelogues until

I pull out a small Polaroid, one of the early ones from the '60s when you still had to coat the surface yourself with fixer.

The shot is of a sharply turned-out black man sitting firmly upright at a table with a half-filled glass of beer in front of him and a saxophone by his side. The suit is pressed and the smile broad—the only thing missing is a porkpie hat, but I guess those had already come and gone by then. But that was the feel of the photo, late '40s early '50s.

Rustling through the box, I see everything is of this same guy: picnicking with his wife, helping his son take his first steps, and, lo and behold, as a younger man, in front of a diner somewhere down in the Chitlin' Circuit, as part of a band—and they're *all* in porkpie hats. I had stumbled across what amounted to an entire life's arc in pictures, contained in nothing bigger than a shoebox.

Before I can ask the guy across the table how he got his hands on something like this, he asks if I know who it is. When I shake my head, he tells me a name I don't recognize, then starts in with the hard sell: the guy's a respected sideman from the '50s and '60s, played on some important records, even made a few of his own until, for reasons unknown, he puts all his belongings in storage and starts driving a truck.

Gives up wherever he's living—his family is probably long-gone—puts whatever he has left that's worth anything in storage and heads back out on the road, only this time in an eighteen-wheeler. As if making a living in the jazz world wasn't hard enough, he's now going to try and make a go of it long-hauling.

Long and short of it, man couldn't pay his storage bill. Which is how this picker came to own it—at an auction of repossessed goods from the storage place. The obvious question is if he knows so much about him, why hasn't he tried to track the guy down to give him (or in this case *sell* him is probably more accurate) back his memories? Most of the pictures would, after all, be far more valuable to the people in them than us pack rats on Canal Street.

His face goes blank—he's not a good Samaritan, he's an alchemist, turning one man's (re)possessions into another's collectible. It's how he makes his living, on the ignorance and/or bad luck, of others. Orchestrating reunions is not part of the job description.

Rankled by my suggestion, he points to my Nikon like it's a fat bank account and asks why *I* don't buy them if I'm so worried about the guy? "What gives you the right to judge?" he keeps repeating, "What gives you the right?"

Nothing. Nothing gives me the right—it just seems like the right thing to do. There are more scoundrels in the world than we care to think about but every time I'm confronted by one it's as if it's for the first time—*I* don't know whether I'm more indignant or incredulous. Color me sentimental, I know, but there was something so unique in that box, so particular to one man, it all seemed far too personal for anyone else to be selling, whether the guy was famous or not.

As the volume of our exchange escalates, I quickly realize my opinion is not of the majority and calling into question one vulture's ethics while surrounded by a bunch of other vultures whose m.o. and moral code is exactly the same probably will mark me as a troublemaker. I decide to try and walk away—buying the box would just encourage him anyway. But this guy won't let it go—he's been shown up in front of his colleagues, by a woman no less, and he has to save face if he expects them to hold him a slot in their parking lot next week and all the weeks thereafter. So he takes after me, still wondering aloud what gives me the right until I weave between a couple of cars and make it to the other side of Canal, disappearing into the throng.

Jazzmen are a cursed lot. When not busy being ripped off by club owners and record companies, they have to deal with people ready to trade on their notoriety. Inside that shoebox was a man's life, all laid out in black-and-white and color, and lost to him through nothing more than a bit of bad luck. I suppose if I really cared I would have taken him at his word, bought the damn thing, and found the guy myself, so maybe I should just shut up about it. Maybe.

### Here, There and Everywhere
November 26, 1980
4:53 P.M.

Walking down W. Broadway late this afternoon I see a caravan of movie trucks parked in front of Sperone—what *now* has landed in our quiet little enclave? The all-white gallery has a white bed draped in white sheets prominently placed in the center of the room. The focal point, however, is a naked-to-the-world couple in the bed, who, if they weren't actually *having* sex, were damn good at faking it. Recording all of this in his stocking feet on the bed was a burly gentleman with an Arri. When finally I get a "full frontal," I realize that what I had stumbled across was not some kind of arch, for-artists-only porn shoot but, in fact, John and Yoko. At it again.

What is it about these two and their need to share their conjugal bed with their public? Is there some kind of not-so-private obsession being worked through here?

Left my cameras at home but visions of album covers danced through my head, nevertheless. Two Virgins Redux or wouldn't that apply anymore?

## More White Rooms

November 29, 1980

11:03 P.M.

After an evening of openings along 57th Street, hopping from one pristine white room to the next, I'm beginning to understand how the gallery scene, at least uptown, is fueled on little more than intimidation and pretension. Is there an over-compensation going on here or simply a crisis in confidence? All these jacked-up, over-designed rooms play as a kind of insurance policy against a show going unsold, a way to tart the work up, to make it appear to be something more than it is.

Which is where the dealers don't understand their business: the work, not the venue, is what should intimidate. Just one more manifestation of that New York neurosis where style is valued over substance, and art is reduced to little more than escapism for the well-heeled individualist. Didn't the rawness of The Times Square Show teach these guys anything?

Made me pine for those openings where art was something you bumped into trying to get another drink. Or was that just sculpture?

### Landlord Blues
November 30, 1980
3:23 P.M.

The landlord was around yet again today, actually the son this time, wondering how much it would take for me to move out. When I asked him where exactly he thought it was I should go, he said he didn't care but if I didn't take his offer now, there might not be another one. He claims B didn't grandfather properly, and therefore I have no right to be using it as a residential space. He's wrong and he knows it. I told him for a $100,000 fixture fee I would consider moving, nothing less.

Forget about the whole heating problem in here, should he persist along these lines I'm thinking I should file some kind of formal complaint with the Loft Board. He's too big and stupid for me to get outright confrontational. He also spends too much time in the Shark Bar, which means he must have "friends" in the neighb who would be only too happy to show me their rap sheets. Perhaps I don't want to shake that tree just yet, for much like our friend the Elephant Man, "I want to live!"

## Imagine

December 9, 1980

2:35 A.M.

Coming home to the Dakota tonight, some time before 11, John Lennon took four bullets in the chest and bled to death in the back of a cop car while his wife looked on from the front seat. It still doesn't seem like I could possibly be writing this—that they're shooting rock stars now—but after seeing the assassin's/fan's prom picture splashed across the front page, the truth of his "accomplishment"— successfully penetrating the headlines and our conscious-ness—speaks louder than anything I might try and tell myself to the contrary.

By the time I was able to make it to the hospital, there already was an outsized pack of press in place. Rather than mill about with the rest of the vipers, I decided to make the long walk home, putting an early end to a night that would have no doubt slid well into morning. So much for journalistic integrity but bed seemed like the only option/antidote. No sleep for the weary of course, but at least I was able to close my eyes and try, however futile the attempt, to forget.

My night had started out at JFK (what shall they name after Lennon?)—Reagan was coming to dine with Kissinger and

Cardinal Cook at Brooke Astor's place. It was to be his first visit to Gotham since being elected, and whoever usually covers such things for the *Post* was unavailable. Jacobs volunteered me even though he knew I had plans, proving once again that editors are little more than mice trained to be rats. In point of fact, going to see *Caligula* on a blind date was a bit too Travis Bickle for me anyway, plus I was happy for the windfall, even if it meant having to look our advancing national fate in the face sooner than I would have liked.

The problem was that the plane was late, making an already cranky press pool increasingly fidgety about meeting their deadlines. All we needed was Bonzo stepping onto the tarmac and making some gesture of acknowledgment—a wave, a smile, whatever—it didn't matter just as long as he was looking vaguely in the direction of the cameras. Little did we know how irrelevant all this would shortly become.

The longer Reagan took to arrive, the more despondent the mood, eventually sending some drifting over to the police barricade where the cops were running a small TV off of a patrol car's cigarette lighter. *Monday Night Football* was on, periodic cheers could be heard. All was right with the New York night. Then everything became very quiet.

I make my way to the cop car only to hear Howard Cossell bearing the bad news. It wasn't until the report came over the police radio—Lennon was en route to Roosevelt Hospital—that we all realized Cossell had it right. Kill the messenger was all I could think.

While my instinct was to go straight to the hospital, leaving before Reagan's arrival was out of the question—I was on assignment, coming back empty-handed was not an option. By the time the president-elect's plane *did* touch down it was almost as an afterthought, dwarfed by the profound sadness that was swelling up among those still remaining on the tarmac.

Walking home from the hospital, I was amazed how many people were wandering the streets, strangers consoling strangers in a daze of disbelief. By the time I got home, hundreds were already holding vigil outside the Dakota. Imagine.

## All God's Chillin' Got Guns
December 14, 1980
11:35 A.M.

Nothing much to put down here—feeling rather emptied actually. Has been less than a week since they shot Beatle John and the fan suicide count is already up to three. To hear the guy who pulled the trigger tell it, Lennon was the phony and this guy is Holden Caufield, self-appointed exterminator of all that is false in the world.

Someone on the radio said they found a Polaroid in Lennon's coat of him signing his new album for his assassin earlier that day. Why couldn't the guy have just taken his trophy and quietly crawled back into his hole like the rest of the obsessives out there?

What can you say without speaking poorly of the dead? The '70s saw Beatle John go from being an architect of an era to a house husband with something to protect (to the tune of $235 mil). Lord knows he hadn't had anything new to say in years (this new one, *Double Fantasy* is a particularly dreary disc), but then great art has never come from contentedness. Why, though, deny the man his domestic bliss and, more to the point, why the death sentence? In the grand scheme, he was at the very least smart enough to know when to sit it out, hungry, demanding fans be damned. Would only Paul have done the same.

This afternoon there was a moment of silence, ten minutes in fact, "for John's soul" as Yoko put it. The whole thing feels larger than just the death of a Very Important Person, and more like a catastrophe, more along the lines of the sinking of the Titanic, in that the ship they said was unsinkable should sink/the man who fashioned himself a peacenik should meet such a violent death. Surely this must be the final nail in the coffin of '60s idealism, the wake-up-and-smell-the-coffee imperative to all those true believers still trying to believe.

The *Post* ran a particularly noxious photo (which, for the *Post*, is saying a lot) on the front page the other day taken of the fallen idol at the morgue just before his body was to be whisked away to a crematorium. Scuttlebutt has it the blood-sucker who took it pocketed $10,000 for his ghoulishness. As someone who has shot in a morgue before, I don't want to sound hypocritical here, but my interest was in death itself, not dead celebrities. If Sontag is right when she says that in

America, photographers don't just record history they invent it, then we as a culture have to hope this is the last time we see this gruesome *momento mori*. (See a picture once it registers, see it twice it's remembered, three times—it's fact.)

Her avant-garde pretenses aside, I was never much of a Yoko fan but I can't help thinking about her and the rest of family he leaves behind. 'Tis a fearful thing to love what death can touch.

Reagan is resuscitated and ready to return us to black & white, while rock stars are now considered fair game, joining the ranks formerly reserved for kings and politicos. These are the beasts and burdens of our time—the cold, hard facts of our lives.

### Another Hour of Darkness
December 20, 1980
4:36 A.M.

Another Hour of Darkness where the noises from the street conspire with the shadows on the walls to create the inexplicable in my already fevered brain. This time it wasn't people fucking across the way, or someone downstairs calling my name but rather the overwhelming sense that somebody was in the room, hovering over me, studying me in all my fits and starts as I tried to sleep. Paranoia or just an acute case of narcissism?

Lately, just before I start to dream, I go into this odd frame of— what to call it . . . meta-consciousness . . . ? where there is no event unfolding, no discernible tense, no past/present/future, it's simply some strange state of pure being where all the truths are self-evident and everything just is what it is. (It sounds ridiculous as I reread this and it *is* ridiculous but there you have it.) And so tonight, just as I am about to leave that state of suspended animation and go into some kind of dream sequence, I keep feeling this "presence" in the room that pulls me out, sends blood rushing to the brain and, presto! I'm awake.

Rather than pull dear diary out and start writing straight away per usual, this time I simply started reading the thing. Not from the beginning, but skipping around, paging to entries at random just to see what I did and didn't like. Maybe it's the hour, or maybe it's just my predisposition toward anything that comes from my own hand but I am beginning to wonder just what the hell I was thinking. Why am I bothering to keep this thing at all? To what end? Chart my progress? What progress? If anything I feel like everything's going sideways—like it's all I can do to even tread water.

Marvin thinks all artists should keep journals—for the history books, he says with the wave of his hand as if I'm being purposefully naïve. And maybe I am. Freud apparently was so disgusted with where his work was going he destroyed everything he had ever written when he was twenty-nine. That's one solution. Not for everyone but then neither was his work.

Let's see what happens in a year when I turn twenty-nine. But where does that leave me now? I'll tell you where: awake and alone at some ungodly hour, staring at the ceiling, that's where!

'80

WINTER

## Lost Gardens
December 23, 1980
5:17 P.M.

Lech has surfaced, with tales to tell per usual. Plato's finally reopened a few weeks back and whoever he attached himself to there took him out to her place in Jersey and kept him out there for days on end. According to Lech, that is.

Apparently the new, improved Plato's was not exactly as marvelous as the regulars had been led to believe. Swinging ain't what it used to be—the city refused the club proper building permits all fall, which is why there have been so many false starts with the opening. Do I smell a Reagan?

According to Lech, the highlight was supposed to be a pool. The city thought otherwise, though, and in order for the club to be allowed to open, the pool had to be drained. The owner covered the bottom in Astroturf and dried shrubbery, trying to give it that Paradise Lost vibe, but apparently the Garden of Eden it was not. More like After the Fall.

Christmas party at Mary and Leon's tonight—together again, for the moment at least. (No comment.) Nothing red to wear but an old raglan sweater left behind by B and slobbered on by Kertesz. Perhaps black would be more appropriate this year anyway. Not feeling very Christmassy, truth be told. Not feeling very much of anything.

# Afterword

The last time I would see M. L. was on December 31, 1980 (one week after her final entry), at a private New Year's Eve fête thrown by yours truly on the roof of the Danceteria nightclub. She was, I can assure you, in a joyous mood that New Year's Eve high atop the city, looking forward to new possibilities in a new decade. And why shouldn't she have been? Her subsequent disappearance and presumed death shocked all who knew her, a loss, the ramifications of which continue to haunt me.

As dispirited as I can become at still having to think of her in the past tense, I *do* find temporary solace in allowing myself the occasional flight-of-fancy as to what may have been her fate. Perhaps one long, blue day she simply shed her old skin and slipped off into another, very different life—farming sheep in New Zealand or celebrity "chefing" under an assumed name in one of Europe's lesser cities. (Bruges often comes to mind, why I know not.) And while she had no *known* affinity for ungulates or fancy foods (or even the Flemish for that matter), maybe such unpredictability is precisely what fuels my idle musings.

The secret, *new* life of M. L. Weeks. A woman not afraid to forge a second act for herself. Privately. Would that we all knew such courage, such humility! She left, after all, no note and other than myself and a few close friends and family, there really wasn't anyone for her to worry about leaving behind. Maybe *that's* what gave her permission to just wake up one morning and disappear. Wishful thinking on my part? Perhaps. But until a body is found this is often how I prefer to think of her.

The days of which M. L. writes, if not necessarily M. L. herself, are gone forever. This diary then, it goes without saying, is as close as one may hope to get in reanimating the spirit of those times—the pure, unadulterated sense of adventure that metabolized them. And with the turn of each sharply-observed page, it is abundantly clear that she was of a breed rarely found in the salt mines of what passes for today's (still) doomed brick and mortar "art world."

Those of us lucky enough to have called her their friend will always cherish her and her many idiosyncrasies, not the least among them being her unstinting generosity of both time and labor.

Long before the *Post* began to devour the hours she once reserved for her portraiture, M. L. was well-known for accommodating her friends' demands for sittings, only to then turn over to them the entire portfolio without demanding so much as her expenses in return. (I personally had the good fortune to be the subject/recipient of two such portfolios, one of which, I am humbled to disclose, is, at the time of publication, soon due to go off at auction in Geneva.) As she herself confirms in these pages, "the business side of this business was never (her) bent."

Thus it is, as the exclusive representative for the Weeks estate that I am exceedingly honored to commemorate the publication of '80 with a *very* limited edition of vintage prints (pencil signed verso). Both seasoned collector and first-time buyer alike now have the opportunity to compete for a piece of art history that, until only recently, had been buried in protracted legal wranglings.

Fortunately for all of us, M. L.'s memory lives on through these vintage prints and, hopefully, her new website. And I think it safe to say that with the publication of these diaries, M. L. will soon (finally) be getting the recognition and acclaim she has so richly deserved and for far too long.

If I have managed to do anything to help prod this new-found interest, it is as little more than enthusiastic proxy for a friend who could not be here to do so herself. As we in gallery circles are fond of asking, Better late than never for your son, eh Mrs. Van Gogh?

Much like certain artists in the Quattro cento who stepped out from the church's shadow in order to create art for art's sake, M. L.'s brazen disregard for the academy and its canon has produced a body of work, which, with few exceptions, knows no real precedent. Now, with the publication of '80, she has managed to make herself in death what she could not have hoped to aspire to in life—*the* keen-eyed archivist of her time. For this, we should all be extremely grateful. I know I am.

Marvin Schagrin
May 2004
www.mlweeks.net